"Elaborate details of the woods, and the quiet, overwhelming powers that both it and being a woman in a patriarchal social structures holds. Bromwich's *At the Edge of the Woods* fits well in a stack with Ottessa Moshfegh's *Death in Her Hands*, but it is also a beautiful, fresh addition to the feminist literary canon."

—**TAY JONES, WHITE WHALE BOOKSTORE**

"Bromwich brilliantly depicts Laura's experience as only that which a woman can have... This is a book to be remembered."

—**JAYLYLL KORRELL, *INDEPENDENT BOOK REVIEW*, STARRED**

"Laura shares her thoughts with the reader on living with nature, interacting with others, and what it means to survive. Beautiful."

—**JILL NAYLOR, NOVEL.**

"This book is an incredible vibe. It's a little bit of Shirley Jackson, a little bit of Virginia Woolf, a little bit of Ottessa Moshfegh and yes, perhaps some Richard Powers for the nature writing..."

—**ANTON BOGOMAZOV, POLITICS & PROSE**

"Intense and hazy, *At the Edge of the Woods* is a feverishly captivating combination of nature writing and character study."

—**MALLORY MELTON, BOOKPEOPLE**

"Earthy, sensuous, and feminist. Through extraordinary nature writing, Bromwich addresses fertility, culture, class, illness, and community. Tense and witchy, this is a story of one woman who lives on her own terms. Glorious."

—**BETH SHAPIRO, SKYLARK BOOKSHOP**

"*At the Edge of the Woods* is a historical yet topical novel about a woman existing outside of society's expectations... Amid lyrical prose and ever-building tension, Laura distances herself from conventional reality, but she may be all the wiser for it."

—**MARY WAHLMEIER, RAVEN BOOK STORE**

At the Edge of the Woods

A NOVEL BY

KATHRYN BROMWICH

Two Dollar Radio
Books too loud to ignore

Two Dollar Radio
Books too loud to Ignore

WHO WE ARE TWO DOLLAR RADIO is a family-run outfit dedicated to reaffirming the cultural and artistic spirit of the publishing industry. We aim to do this by presenting bold works of literary merit, each book, individually and collectively, providing a sonic progression that we believe to be too loud to ignore.

TwoDollarRadio.com

Proudly based in

Columbus
OHIO

 @TwoDollarRadio

 @TwoDollarRadio

 /TwoDollarRadio

Love the
PLANET?
So do we.

Printed on Rolland Enviro.
This paper contains 100% post-consumer fiber, is manufactured using renewable energy - Biogas and processed chlorine free.

Printed in Canada

 100% **PCF**   BIO GAS ENERGY   PERMANENT

SOME RECOMMENDED LOCATIONS FOR READING:
Pretty much anywhere because books are portable and the perfect technology!

AUTHOR PHOTO⟶
Alice Zoo

COVER PHOTO⟶ Photo by Sergei Sviridov on Unsplash
DESIGN⟶ Eric Obenauf

Two Dollar Radio acknowledges that the land where we live and work is the contemporary territory of multiple Indigenous Nations.

For my parents

A forest knows things. They wire themselves up underground. There are brains down there, ones our own brains aren't shaped to see. Root plasticity, solving problems and making decisions. Fungal synapses. What else do you want to call it? Link enough trees together, and a forest grows aware.

Richard Powers, *The Overstory*

I am like a dog—smells excite me... The earthy smell of moss, and the soil itself, is best savoured by grubbing... But eye and touch have the greatest potency for me. The eye brings infinity into my vision.

Nan Shepherd, *The Living Mountain*

At the Edge of the Woods

I

1

In the mornings, when my thoughts have not yet arranged themselves into their familiar malevolent shapes and the day is still unformed, I wake up before dawn and sheathe myself in layer upon layer of coarse, heavy clothing, and walk deep into the woods while my eyes adjust to the velvety darkness. In time I have learned the path's duplicitous ways—its thorns and unsteady footholds and half-seen creatures have become better known to me lately than my own reflection, which with the passing of the years has departed so much from the image I expect to see staring back that steeling myself to face it has become a daily penance, a source of horror so visceral and intense that for the ensuing minutes it taints all other considerations. But in the trees here there are no mirrors, or others in whose glances I can see myself reflected, only the astringent cold stinging my eyes and the soft sweet smell of growth and decay.

As I walk my blood runs warm through my veins and my body starts to sweat, and within minutes I need to remove the first layer, which I fumble to tie around my waist underneath my leather bag. My muscles guide me through the branches and into an opening, the grass high and rough against my legs, and the first signs of light begin to glimmer in the sky, the starry blackness fading to a dark gray. I have a sip of water, chilled and scratchy against the back of my throat, and walk to the end of the path, where the steps begin. The first fifteen minutes are some of the steepest and so I pace myself, ensuring my boots have gripped onto each cracked wooden slat before moving to the next, and while it now takes me longer to become out of breath than the first time I did this walk all those months ago, here is where I get the first ferrous tang of blood in my mouth. I stop at a platform to look back at the view starting to be visible below, while I remove another layer and eat half a pastry, stale from the day before, which dissolves into a sugary paste that masks the bitter metallic aftertaste.

The next half hour is an arduous and constant uphill climb. Some days this is where other early-morning hikers come into view, aging mountaineers intoning "buongiorno" or the occasional startled villager. I have come to recognize a few regulars, often so deep in thought that they—as I expect I must—appear lost in a faraway realm, and we pass each other in silence with a perfunctory nod. I try not to imagine the version of me they see, all matted fabric and dirt and ill-concealed truculence, and march on, the hard ground crunching beneath me like gravel. At the top of the steps the paths widen out and it becomes once again easy to disappear into the forest without encountering anyone, a moment that fills me each day with immense relief. At this stage the adrenaline has started to kick in, overpowering the soreness in my legs and the stiffness in my joints, and as I make my way off the path and weave through the overgrown thicket, my thoughts at last begin to disperse. Often, a snippet of a phrase I read the previous night will get stuck in my head, repeating over and over like an incantation until the words have lost all meaning.

This is where I eat the second half of the pastry, which sits warm and satisfying in my stomach; I can feel it become fuel almost instantly as it descends, replenishing the energy I have used during the morning's climb. Not long afterward, I will normally feel the need to relieve myself in a secluded corner of the woods, something that at first filled me with great shame but which I now regard as an animalistic ritual I enact without much thought yet not without relish. I clean myself with paper I have brought with me; if I run out, I have learned which leaves to use and which to avoid. The dangers latent in the mountain, at first masked by its majestic grandeur, have slowly revealed themselves to me; I am more fearful of it now, but wiser to the ways it conceals its threats. If I do not disturb it, I think, it will allow me to pass unharmed.

As I proceed up through the forest, I try not to retread my steps, each day tracking a new pathway through the undergrowth, but time and time again I find myself heading to one of three endpoints I have come to favor. Once I reach the top of the pass, I stop to consider the view beneath me. Sometimes, I gaze over the peaks, the trees, the lake in the distance, the gossamer clouds billowing out in bruises of blue and pink, purple and gold, the horizon a clear gleam like a lamp shining behind a pale yellow veil, branches snaking in front of it like the centerpiece of a stained glass window, and the view fills me with awe, with the sense of being fully alive and as though the beauty in the world might, after all, make up for its endless disappointments; once or twice, the sight has left me lost for words, breathless, as though I might be approaching something meaningful but just out of reach. Most days, I look down, my feet aching and calloused, sweat coalescing on my back and armpits and groin, my throat dry and raw with exertion, and I feel nothing at all.

2

Back in the village, I make myself smaller, softer, amenable to human interaction. I change into neat, clean clothes and widen my mouth into a smile, which I practice in the mirror until it is meek and becoming. I feel myself once again turning into the docile girl I was brought up to be, a performance I find both calming and degrading. I greet the butcher's assistant and the tavern boy and they respectfully nod in my direction, unsure where to direct their gaze. As I pass them I rehearse in my head the small talk I will attempt with the shopkeeper, whose usual mode of address to me communicates both obsequiousness and an undercurrent of disdain, a demeanor he adopts toward all things unfamiliar to him. In time, I think, I will win him over, even if it takes until every hair on my head has turned to gray. Once I am old, the kind of old that makes the young and healthy turn away, our encounters will be seamless, routine; intimate, almost—if I ever break through to his carefully guarded inner circle of clientele, that is.

"Morning, miss." A cheerful singsong, thick black moustache leering over fleshy lips. "And how are we today?" Ostensibly polite words, yet delivered in a tone so steeped in reverence as to imply the very opposite. He thinks I don't know what he's doing, but I've seen him with his favored customers: patter honed over decades into a smooth barrage of in-jokes and mutual insults, not at all like this specious performance.

"All right, Gianfranco." Casual, but aloof enough to denote that I've perceived his discourtesy. "Had an early start, managed to get up to the pass before ten. How about yourself?" I know his game. I am giving nothing away.

"Oh you know." He puffs up with a theatrical display of stoicism. "The usual complaints. What can I do you for today?" The same lubricious line every time, the same flicker of loathing commingled with lust.

I give him my order: cured ham, tinned fish, eggs, bread, pastries, two bottles of red wine. I watch him as I order the wine, daring him to comment on it, as he did the first few times.

"Naturally, m'lady," he slithers, unctuous as an eel. His meaty fingers move quickly and skillfully through the products, squeezing and weighing and slicing and wrapping until everything is packed together in a brown paper bag, which he passes over the counter to me. I settle up and flash him my kindest smile; I am no threat to you, this smile says. A few more years of these and he will come around to me, I am certain of it.

I emerge from the shop and into the street, slick with rain from an unexpected shower that broke out as I approached the village. The paving stones reflect the sun into my eyes and I instinctively close them for a few seconds, breathing in the dampness in the air. I cross into the piazza, where the fruit and vegetable carts are packing up for the morning and women are setting up stalls with flowers and dusty bric-a-brac: old dolls, picture frames, lopsided jewelry. I wave at a few familiar faces with my spare hand, the paving slabs smooth and treacherous under my feet. The stench of wet horse manure comes through in waves, weaving between the sweet aroma from the bakery and the pile of discarded vegetables spoiling in the sun.

I turn down the side street next to the church and start my ascent toward the outskirts, passing the pharmacy on the way. The houses here become smaller, their angles increasingly precarious, the passers-by more infrequent and lugubrious with every corner I pass. Although everything appears calm and orderly, in these streets I find myself momentarily filled with a dull dread, as though those around me were congregating for a funeral, the church bells tolling thuddingly behind me.

Within a few minutes I arrive at the stream that marks the outer limit of the village; past the bridge I can see the Rossettis' farm, their brown mastiff starting his customary cacophony of aggression whenever I come near. I tighten my grip on the bag and hurry past, my feet firmer now on the rough ground, dank and reassuringly grainy.

"Good boy, Bruno," I repeat over and over, in a tone not dissimilar to the one I used in the shop earlier. "Who's a good boy?" Tilting his wrinkled head to one side, Bruno stops barking, sniffs the air, and resumes with renewed ferocity.

After the farm I pass through the field leading into the woods, where the incline steepens. To the right is a dirt track weaving through the trees; I exhale as I leave the morning behind, allowing the smile to dissolve from my face. My feet move automatically, spurred by a newfound reserve of energy. I step into the shade as the birdsong surrounds me, lizards scurrying away as I approach. The branches creak as though to welcome me back, the leaves dappling the sunlight like fine embroidery. I walk along the path until it forks into two; I turn left onto the neglected passageway that leads into the clearing where my lodgings are.

When I first tried to rent the cabin, the landlord refused to countenance it: this is no place for a woman to live alone, he insisted—far too isolated, more of a hut than a house, not safe at all. After much wrangling, a discreet gratuity and the assurance that my husband was due to join me at any moment, the elderly man relented, on the proviso that I stop by his palazzo once a month to give him an update on how I'm getting along, a trip I never embark on empty-handed. If the villagers whisper about the arrangement, they do so out of earshot.

The previous tenant, a former soldier of few words and dubious provenance, had left it in a state of disrepair, departing suddenly after a gruesome hunting accident. Accounts vary: some say his rifle went off as he was walking and destroyed part of his foot, others believe he blinded himself in one eye after attempting to take his own life, others still that he mistook someone for a deer and buried the body in the woods. Either way, his name is only ever uttered in a hoarse whisper, as if telling ghost stories to a group of children assembled around a fireplace. Most of the time, he is referred to simply as *il mostro*.

3

The cabin is not much to look at from the outside. It's a plain rectangular building with windows on three sides and dilapidated brown wooden shutters; the walls are rough-hewn and uneven, light gray bricks that slant subtly in uncertain directions. The gable roof, a gap-toothed patchwork of faded slate tiles, ends in a rickety gutter mottled with rust. A decrepit tree, pale and gnarly like the hands of my grandmother when I was small, seems to be leaning across the front window for support. A steady stream of ants emanates from, and disappears into, a crack on the back wall.

But once I was allowed inside for the first time, it was as though my mind had been emptied of all its noise, its peculiar obsessions, and filled with pure silence. I stood inside the darkened room, air thick with the smells and left-behind clutter of its previous inhabitant, and felt as if a balm had been applied to my inner being. The cool shade, the noises of the forest, the smooth ceramic tiles of the floor: I was flooded with memories from many years before, of a school trip to the seaside when I had broken away from the group and found an abandoned shack on the beach. I hid for hours before they found me, lying on the filthy ground and singing softly to myself, my teachers frenzied with anger and relief.

It took several weeks to clear the wreckage left behind by the soldier: old clothes, crumbling papers, mildew, residues of rotten food, stains of inexplicable shades. I spent sweaty afternoons scrubbing away the profanities, declarations of love and cryptic affirmations that strangers had scrawled onto the walls in the interim between our leases. I picked up the dead leaves and branches in the clearing that surrounds the house, pruned the overgrown plants and shrubs, and assiduously tended to the pale tree, even though it continues to show no sign of life.

Eventually, my living quarters were complete: a studio room with a washbasin and single bed to the side, a basic kitchen near the front door, and opposite the stove a table that doubles as dining area and desk. In the village I picked up two small bookcases, a chair, two kerosene lamps and some woolen blankets; I keep the few clothes I brought with me in the same trunk I used to travel here. The light streams in from the east in the mornings, imbuing everything with a crisp brilliance, while afternoons are golden, lazy, the shutters keeping out the rising heat while letting through glimmers of sun. Walking in after an absence, the room always appears to me spare and tidy and precise; the one element of chaos comes from the books, scattered haphazardly on the bed and desk.

A rudimentary squat toilet can be reached outside, in a wooden shack under cover of the trees. In the beginning I would lay in bed, stifling my urges, to avoid walking out into the cold darkness. The first time I made my way to the outhouse at night, the full moon illuminated the clearing so that everything appeared bathed in a wash of blue, alchemically transformed. The noises of the forest were louder, fiercer, less wary of my presence; some shuffling I recognized as a thrush or rabbit, other sounds were more ambiguous. After that it became easier, to the extent that I now look forward to my nocturnal outings, the murmurs around me a tranquil and nonchalant chorus.

My meals are simple, due both to taste and necessity. I eat little and often, hard cheese on bread, pieces of fruit, steering clear of cooked meals so as to minimize trips into the village. I remember a few recipes that my mother taught me when I was younger, but my skills are limited; it has been a long time since I have had to cook for myself. Over the past year, through trial and error, I have developed a handful of quick dishes I turn to time and again, combining the local ingredients with the tastes I became accustomed to during my marriage. Living on my own, my needs have become almost spartan; gone are the seemingly insatiable appetites of my youth, when no dessert was too sweet, no sauce too rich, when as soon as one feast was finished I would begin to contemplate the next.

*

Once I have put my provisions away, I wash myself using a basin of water which has warmed in the sun during my absence. I use a cloth to rub myself, the mud and sweat coming off to reveal pink scrubbed skin underneath, the water in the bowl turning darker as I go. I lie in the sun for a few minutes to let the water drip off, a thin towel wrapped around my torso. Once I am mostly dry, I go back into the house and lower myself onto the creaky bed, where I sleep a deep and dreamless sleep for an hour as the sun blazes restlessly outside.

In the afternoon, I have a light lunch and set about my work. Where I can I pick up the odd commission from locals who need documents and letters translated from or into French: the apothecary and doctor give me irregular but well-remunerated assignments, which I struggle through using a medical dictionary. When the translation work dries up, I head into the village to tutor the more affluent locals' children in languages, science and classics. With the money I have left and my meager expenses, I can get by with just a few hours of work a day—a reasonable exchange, yet I find myself increasingly resentful of this relentless interruption of my daily rituals.

Later in the evening, when the heat has subsided to a manageable level, I head back down to the fork in the path and turn to the right. I walk uphill for five minutes until I get to the old well, where I fill my bucket with pristine water, so cold and fresh that

I drink several mouthfuls on the spot. Occasionally someone from the farm will be there, but most of the time I am alone. I carry the heavy bucket back to the cabin and decant half of it into two glass bottles that I will use for drinking; the other half I put aside for ablutions.

This is when I pour myself the first drink of the day, a glass of red wine that I sip little by little, letting its anesthetic effect wash over me in waves. I slice some cheese and prosciutto and eat it with bread and sliced tomatoes, followed by an apricot or apple. If it is a cold evening I put some logs in the stove in the corner of the room, which emanates a sputtering, unsteady heat. After dinner I fill my glass again, to the brim this time, and I sit down to read by the light of the lamp.

After the dense and unflinchingly logical texts I read during the day—medical journals for my translations, newspapers I pick up in the village—now is the time for me to turn to matters that disturb my thoughts in pleasurable ways. I spend the following hours reading strange, subversive novels by tortured Russian existentialists, Gothic stories in which there is no division between life and death, mystical poems that reconfigure reality to their will, Eastern scriptures, political and philosophical treatises that call for revolution in thought and action—books which, in my previous life, I had carefully concealed from my husband's watchful gaze.

Sometimes, if I have stayed up beyond the point where my thoughts start to untether themselves from reason, I turn to the drawer I keep locked when I leave the house: arcane religious texts, parapsychology, French occultism. During the day, it is easy to distance myself from the books' more esoteric conclusions, but when I am alone, surrounded by the sounds of the forest at night, my mind loosened by laudanum and cheap wine, I feel as though I have stepped over a threshold, passed from a place of dreariness into somewhere new, dangerous, that I don't fully understand.

4

An incomplete compendium of incidents I have observed while on my walks:

A bird of prey flying overhead in ever-smaller circles, hovering before hurtling toward the ground; a sound of rustling in the dark; it emerges holding a vole in its beak, which squeaks violently as the bird soars back into the sky.

A pine marten at the other end of a field, jumping and writhing in the sun with insect-like agility; a second one appears and they chase each other at an impossible speed, a manic blur of yellow and brown; the moment I tread on a branch, they disappear.

A broken bottle, which I don't see until I've stepped on it; one shard goes straight through the sole of my boot, puncturing my skin. As I attempt to disentangle the glass from the leather, I cut my fingers; I wrap my hand with a handkerchief, which becomes so bloodied and stiff I later bury it in the ground.

Clouds rapidly rising up the side of the mountain, so white and thick they appear to be solid; as they ascend, they expand and soften, enveloping the peaks in wraithlike shrouds before dissolving into the sun.

A scrawny wolf, just about visible in the distance across the plateau; she is lying on the ground, motionless. I strain my eyes to see whether I can detect breathing, but her thorax appears still, deflated. By the time I have walked toward her through the woods, she is gone.

Meadows full of wildflowers, stretching along the green expanse in bursts of cobalt, ivory, gold, carmine. From a distance, the color is rich, uniform; as I approach, the heavy clusters thin out in the grass, a crumbling mirage.

The remnants of a campfire, translucent smoke still rising from it; nearby are discarded chicken bones and grease-stained paper, ants and flies congregating on them as if partaking in a sumptuous meal.

Human and animal excreta; some hidden in bushes or under leaves, occasionally out in the open; too numerous to count.

A family of ibex climbing a rock face; they move nimbly, hooves hard against the ground, appearing to float as they rise and rise, impervious to the laws of gravity.

A young couple, locked in an embrace; when they see me, the girl cries out and hides her face while the boy, eyeing me with animosity, puts his arms around her; as I walk away, I hear them laughing to themselves.

Down by the well, a baroque curl, no bigger than my fingernail—is it moss, or lichen?—growing on the inside of the wall. As I lean forward to get a better look at the carnation-colored spiral, the light changes and it is hidden in shadow.

The body of a rabbit, long dead, its flesh decomposing in the warm sun. At first I turn away but find my gaze drawn to it again, inspecting the ways in which skin and fur have given way to a putrid, gleaming surface, tiny white maggots burrowing gently into the carcass.

A shrine under an enormous oak tree, out of sight from the closest path: twigs, stones, leaves and petals arranged in careful patterns; in the center is a pile of sticks, tied together at the top like a tepee, with an opening on one side. I peer inside to find that it has been filled with fine pebbles and dried flowers.

An elderly man holding himself up against a tree, a pained expression on his face; as I glance over he turns toward me, revealing his other arm manically working his genitals, an angry flash of pink I avert my eyes from; too late.

5

Once a week, I warm up some water on the stove and use it to wash myself with a bar of soap. I wrap my wet hair in a towel and lie back on an ancient fallen log outside the cabin, reading and smoking cigarettes in the sun. The pine trees surrounding the clearing look bright and strong in the early afternoon light, their deep greenness emanating the promise of shade for when the heat becomes too intense. Birds and small animals wander around their roots, pausing when they become aware of my presence. I have learned to glance away and make myself still when this happens, so that they resume their inscrutable missions as before, occasionally darting their eyes back to me.

If I am going into the village, I do my best to smooth out the more feral edges that have started to manifest in me. I suspect that the villagers tolerate my unusual living arrangements due to an assumption that my background is somewhat genteel, and to the fact that I am educated, which they both distrust and defer to; not being familiar with the local dialect, I communicate in standard Italian, another marker of difference. In order to continue in this state of mutual understanding, I endeavor to maintain a veneer of respectability: cleanliness, manners, a subdued demeanor toward men. To make up for the fact that I do not attend church, I make sure to regularly stop by and exchange a few pleasantries with the priest, telling him about which birds I have spotted on my walks, as well as making a modest contribution to the alms box.

One afternoon, I take a deep breath before inspecting my reflection in the small mirror by the bed, my eyes scrupulously noting each new imperfection. Since my arrival here, I have dispensed with the expensive and time-consuming beauty rituals I observed in the past, the ointments and oils, powders and pomades. When I was a girl, I had looked forward to this stage of my life: my wrinkles would be distinguished, I had thought, like creases on crepe paper, a sign of the experiences that had marked me. Instead, my face has become lined with deep, aggressive furrows, its sleek oval distorted into that of a stranger, perpetually embittered by anger or fatigue. I am not yet forty, so more changes are still to come: the signs on my face and body merely indicate where the ravages of time will make their mark.

But, during this time, what I have lost in grace I have gained in strength. My limbs have become hard and lean, initial sunburns peeling away delicate layers of skin to reveal a golden-brown surface, coarse and durable like leather; my blue eyes are luminous against my newly bronzed face. My dark hair, streaked with threads of silver, has grown thick and long, liberated after decades of grooming and braiding. Although the years have transformed me, remnants of my beauty flash through on occasion; I can see it in the eyes of the village's women more clearly than those of its men. On some instinctive level, I am aware that I must use its power wisely, before it leaves me altogether. If I move to another village once those flashes have gone, I'll have a different power, that of invisibility.

My nickname in town among a certain kind of man, those who don't even attempt to disguise their leers, is *la bella forestiera*, the beautiful foreigner: a compliment they mean as benign, but which continually reminds me of my status as outsider. While I was born in this country, after my marriage I moved across the border to France, returning only intermittently. During those years, something happened to my sense of self: I lost touch with who I used to be, my once-clear identity gradually falling away. Yet I never succeeded in enmeshing myself fully in my new culture: my tongue was too slow, my vowels wrong, my references unfamiliar. And, by the time I returned to the country I once called home, I no longer belonged there, either.

That evening, as the summer days grow shorter and the air is tinged with dusk, I open the cupboard and inspect what's left of the wine. I pour out a glass and drain it in two long sips, and when it becomes apparent that this will be insufficient I comb my hair and make my preparations to go out. By now I am known to enough people in the village as not to elicit the curious, lingering stares I was subjected to when I first arrived; still, I tend to avoid leaving the house after dark, when the niceties of the day become hazier. Tonight, I can see no alternative.

As I approach the bridge, nightfall is closing in on the tilted roofs, windows flickering with candlelight. The familiar streets appear simultaneously more tranquil and secretive at this time, as though I had accidentally wandered into a different town. I walk as if with no destination in mind, inspecting the faces around me: a mother fussing over a girl whose bonnet has come undone; young people engrossed in each other, their movements sudden and unpredictable; a woman with a slight limp gripping her husband's hand; tradesmen laughing raucously. In the main square, groups of varying sizes have gathered around the tables of the two main cafés, drinking dark, bitter spirits amid cloying clouds of cigar smoke. A commotion is underway in front of the town hall, where a stage is being set up: men are transporting planks of wood, shouting to each other over the hammering. Children mill about, the rowdy construction work giving their games a renewed sense of chaos.

As I pass the café on the south of the piazza, speeding up my footsteps on the way to the shop, I hear the sound of my name coming from one of the tables. I turn around, trying to place the voice's owner.

"Signora Mantovani," I hear again, and my eyes land on the face of the apothecary, an extraordinary amount of teeth filling his smile.

"Signor Barbieri," I say, impulsively mirroring his expression back at him. "Signora Barbieri," I add, turning toward his wife, who is pulling out a chair next to her. My tone implies they are the very people I was hoping to meet tonight; inside, I am incensed with them for obstructing my plan.

Hearing my name in this village always startles me. I do not wear a wedding ring, so there is some confusion as to whether I should be addressed as *signora* or *signorina*; most err on the side of *signora*, evidently seen as the more respectful option. Since coming here, I have reverted to my mother's maiden name, which compounds the sense of disorientation.

I take a seat next to the couple, who have become flustered in their attempt to move their chairs further apart to make room for mine.

"There we go," exhales the wife, sitting straight and rearranging a stray lock of hair. She is an elegant woman of about forty, with neat auburn ringlets arranged around her face and the scrupulous manner of someone who runs a tremendously efficient household. "Make yourself comfortable."

"Quite a racket they're making over there," I say as I take my seat, gesturing with my eyes toward the stage being assembled.

"Quite," agrees the apothecary, scratching his silvery beard. "It's for the festival," he adds, as though he's stating the obvious.

His wife, noting the consternation on my face, jumps in. "She doesn't know," she sighs, as though that is just as obvious. She turns to me and, with the delivery of a schoolteacher, explains, "La festa di Santa Maria delle Grazie. Next Saturday. It's a big celebration for the village: there's food, and drink, and music, and little trinkets you can buy." Her eyes start to glisten with emotion. "At midnight there's a competition to see which of the local men is the strongest: they put a tin crown at the top of the tallest tree in the forest and they race to see who gets it first." She turns to her husband, with an expression that tells me he is not a past winner.

"It's *great* fun," agrees the apothecary, who either has not noticed or is not acknowledging the barb. "You must come."

"I'll see if I can make it," I say, amused by the idea of consulting a busy diary.

"Thank you again for all your work with Alberto and Enrico," interjects Mrs Barbieri. "Their writing has improved im-meas-ur-ab-ly," she enunciates. "It really is so delightful to consort with other learned people—unusual, in this village." She gazes around the square and makes a show of displeasure, a swift departure from her misty-eyed look a minute ago. "But of course," she adds with a conspiratorial air, "you must be used to much finer company than this, where you're from."

"Oh," I start, wondering what exactly she has heard about where I'm from. "You know. It's a wonderful village—everyone has been very kind to me."

"Naturally, dear," she nods without conviction. "But forgive my manners—let us get you a drink. What would you like?"

I glance down at their table to make a quick judgement: they are sharing a modest carafe of rosé wine. My thirst feels ravenous in that instant, but I start to wonder whether drinking in front of my sometime-employers would be advisable, and before I've come to a conclusion she has snapped her fingers at the waiter, bidding him to come. I long to be back in my cabin.

Seconds later, the waiter has approached the table; I look up with contrition. He is studying me with an inscrutable expression, seemingly amused by the whole situation. He has thick, curly dark hair and intense eyes, and is so handsome I can barely look at him.

A pause. "What can I get for you?" The Barbieris' eyes are burning into me. I wish I could disappear into thin air.

"A—" I begin, not at all certain where the sentence is going next. "A glass of red wine?" I hate this version of myself.

"Of course." He holds my gaze for a fraction too long, then looks away and smiles.

6

The following Saturday, I lie in the sun, telling myself I will not be attending the village festival. There is an oppressive heat in the air, a heaviness that usually presages rain. Droplets from my damp hair are falling onto my shoulders and torso, cooling my body in a way too localized to be entirely agreeable; I shiver slightly, while the ground scorches my toes.

After so long in near-confinement, my evening with the Barbieris had left me drained of energy for the ensuing days. I am tentative to attend a large gathering; the idea of masses of bodies in close proximity fills me with a kind of revulsion. I shall stay here, I think, and cook myself a dinner of *pollo alla cacciatora*, a rather lavish recipe compared to my usual fare. The next time I go into town, everyone will surely tell me all about the festivities.

As evening approaches, a soft noise starts to emanate from below, a dull hum or buzzing indicating an increase in activity. I read for a while, then tidy the clothes and books scattered around the room. I feel a pang of hunger so I set about preparing my meal: I chop onions, carrots and celery, and put aside the rosemary, garlic and tomatoes I will need later. I open the storage cabinet and take out the chicken, which I unwrap on the counter. As soon as the paper encasing is removed, a stench fills my nostrils and I suppress a retch, hurriedly wrapping the spoiled meat again. I stuff it back in its bag, take it outside and throw it in the woods; a feast for the ants.

The distant din of music and laughter is growing louder. I try to block it out but something is starting to stir within me, fragmented echoes of the parties I had once enjoyed losing myself in. These days I live much more in my memories; my life is quieter but my thoughts are louder, and there is not room for both. I find that the smallest thing—a line of poetry, a scent—will bring to mind a short, intense impression of a specific moment in the past, a particular place; these recollections flash inside me for an instant, as vivid as if they were happening for the first time, before disappearing again just as fast, leaving behind only a lingering sense of melancholy. If I try to recall them for longer, or in greater detail, they soften and distort until they do not feel right anymore, so that every time I revisit them they seem to have shifted a little—they are delicate things, and must not be tampered with too much.

As I listen to the hum pooling into the clearing, my chest tight with bittersweet memories of friends I might never see again, I am flooded with a deep, sudden longing for the company of others. I know that, if I am left alone, I won't be able to listen to that noise all night without my thoughts turning to the past, to everything that happened. To distract myself I start to get ready for the evening, a ritual so familiar it instantly puts my mind at ease, focusing instead on the many small tasks necessary to embellish my appearance: hair, jewels, the finest dress I own. Once I am satisfied with the result, I lock the door and head down with a kerosene lamp, which I will stow at the start of the path and later retrieve on the way home.

As I pass the Rossettis' farm, it becomes clear that the streets are filled with far more people than I had envisaged. I cross over the bridge and find that my usual way into the village has been occupied by stalls, each of which is surrounded by several customers and seemingly as many stallholders. I take a detour, passing by the school, and find that the street is nearly as busy, though a little wider. I begin to make my way through, stepping around groups huddled around shops, outside houses, spilling off the pavement and onto the cobbled streets.

I notice face after face I have never seen before, which unsettles me; the accents that fill the air appear different from the one I've become accustomed to hearing. People from the neighboring towns and hamlets must have come for the night, to sell their wares, to meet friends and relatives, to assuage an assortment of appetites. I walk past some unfamiliar men, and I am glad I do not understand the dialect in which they call out.

When I get to the piazza, a throng has gathered around the wooden platform in front of the town hall. A middle-aged man is singing an upbeat, rhythmic song, and two children in traditional dress are folk dancing around him on the stage, the crowd clapping in unison with the beat. Around the fountain in the middle of the square, a dozen young people exchange pointed words and looks, calculating the group's hierarchies and shifting loyalties. Nonnas in black garments sit around tables, slapping their hands on their knees as grandchildren dance around them, parents gazing amorously into each other's eyes. Gianfranco is there with his wife, clutching half-drunk glasses of wine; he holds her close to him as they sway to the music.

As the sky fades to a dark purple, the nearby houses' windows start to emanate a warm glow; oil lamps, wall-mounted lanterns and candles bathe faces in gold. The sides of the piazza are filled with yet more stalls, which I inspect as I maneuver myself toward the front: farmers selling olives, jams and pickles; perfumed soap and bunches of dried lavender; garish watercolors of pastoral idylls. At the back of the square, a rival folk singer is adding his voice to the mix, strumming a guitar for a cluster of people who erupt into an impromptu dance.

The music on stage comes to an end and a man is making an announcement, barely audible from where I am standing. Starting from the front, the crowd steps aside, creating a thoroughfare among the assembled bodies, an expectant silence falling upon the scene. Nothing seems to happen for a few minutes, during which the murmur of conversation starts to burble up again, until we hear, and then see, a marching band approaching from behind the platform, emerging from the general direction of the church. The men come into view in dazzling green and yellow uniforms, brass instruments filling the air with noise, the earth vibrating with the pulse of their drums. Next come flower girls in sugared-almond-pink dresses, bashfully showering handfuls of petals from pale wicker baskets, both intimidated and emboldened by the tumult around them.

Once the girls have passed, sharp rows of soldiers step in precise, heavy synchrony, identical in starched blue jackets and lacquered belts, helmets fastened tight and low over their faces. The clergy come next, in long, ornate robes and beatific smiles. They are arranged in a square formation around a carrier holding the centerpiece of the procession: a statue of a Madonna and child dyed in ostentatious reds and greens, framed by an elaborate golden arch. The Virgin Mary is carrying baby Jesus in one hand, and in the other an object I can't quite make out. I peer at the woman beside me, who is clasping her hands to her chest, and I ask if she knows what it is. She scrutinizes me with distrust before telling me that the mother of God is holding a nail from the holy cross, then returns to her rapturous appraisal.

After the clergy comes a disparate congregation of bystanders, who have joined in behind the procession and now follow in their footsteps. Once they have dispersed, the music starts up again from the stage; having admired the holy nail, the mass of people return to their dancing and embraces, energized by the display. I study the piazza for faces I recognize: I see a police officer exchanging a joke with the doctor, the butcher catching up with two rubicund farmers. It is apparent that they, and those around them, have been drinking for several hours now.

As the hubbub around me swells, I realize I am light-headed; it has been hours since I've eaten anything. I turn around, searching for a place where the crowd thins out; the back of the square is quieter, so I fight my way through until I can breathe more freely. In the corner I spy what I am looking for, and gravitate toward the café that I have been trying not to think about all night.

7

Compared to the rest of the square, the café appears calm, almost sedate, but it is far busier than the last time I visited. The tables are thrumming with customers, the clientele marginally more distinguished than that of the café near the stage. Further up the road, the village tavern throbs with noise, every now and then emitting outbursts of shouting so loud that some of the café's patrons turn around in alarm, before tutting in amused disapproval with their companions.

Now that I've become aware of my hunger, it is all-encompassing; I feel dizzy and weak, my throat raw with thirst. I scan the crowd for the Barbieris, who thankfully are not present; a lanky, pale-faced boy is waiting tables tonight. I see that some of the customers have plates in front of them, so I turn to the back of the café, where there is a counter serving food. Behind the counter, tending the bar, is the curly-haired waiter from the other day.

I hesitate. It is true that I had secretly been hoping to see him again tonight, but the sudden prospect of the encounter fills me with timidity. All night, I have been assessing myself against the village's women, methodically scanning faces and bodies for flaws and advantages. Even taking into account the distaste I feel when I look in the mirror, I must admit that the comparison is largely favorable, with the exception of a handful of girls in the prime of youth, wearing their beauty like armor.

I start to walk toward the bar—in any case, I think, I need to apologize for our last meeting. As I approach, the waiter glances up and sees me, nodding in greeting as he pours a drink for a thick-figured man. There is something in his expression that suggests he is not entirely surprised I have returned, which annoys me, but at the same time quickens my pulse.

While he finishes up with the other customers I inspect the food on offer: panini, fried dough parcels, stuffed olives. I am hungry, but too nervous to eat.

I feel his eyes on me before I hear his voice. "How can I help?"

I look up, smile, and he smiles back. I order a small piece of focaccia, some water and a glass of wine, suppressing the tremor of nervousness threatening to creep into my voice.

"I'm sorry about the other day," I say while he's preparing my order. "I tutor the Barbieris' children, I had to—"

He laughs, shaking his head. "Don't worry about it. It's not your fault signora Barbieri is a monster." He looks around the bar, eyeing a gentleman behind me who has been vociferously complaining for the past few minutes. "I'm used to that sort of thing. But thank you."

A customer beckons, so he disappears for a few minutes while I gulp down the water and eat a few bites of bread, warm and fragrant with rosemary. Another bartender, an older man who appears to be the proprietor, comes out from the kitchen and helps with the drinks, joining a conversation with a rowdy group at the other end of the bar.

In a quiet moment, the dark-haired waiter comes over and clears away my empty glass of water, then leans his elbows against the bar.

"What do you make of the festival, then?" he asks casually; he has done this before.

"Busy," I hedge my bets, trying to gauge his feelings about it. "The procession was impressive." I refrain from asking his thoughts on the holy nail.

"Are you going to watch the climbing of the tree later?" he asks, a smile playing about his lips.

"I don't think so," I laugh. He is tall, I note, with a strong build. "Will you be taking part?"

"No," he frowns slightly. "I'm not, you know, a *local*," he stresses the final word in an uncertain way. Seeing the question on my face, he adds, "My family is from the South. I moved here when I was seventeen, looking for work."

"I see." He appears to be three or four years younger than me; if he still hasn't been accepted in town after all this time, there is little hope for me.

"Before I moved here I used to hate Northerners," he continues, picking up a glass from behind the counter and drying it. I wonder if he is this forthright with all his customers; I worry that someone else will hear him.

"Do you still?" My voice is quiet among the chatter, so that he has to lean closer.

"Some of them are all right," he smiles. "You're not from around here." A statement rather than a question.

"No—I grew up on the Adriatic coast." I'm not sure why I'm telling him this; I hadn't planned to. "I lived in France for a while."

"Hence the accent," he replies, which irritates me, though he seems to mean it as a compliment. "Well, pleasure to meet you…"

"Laura."

"Vincenzo." He reaches out his hand to shake mine. His grip feels powerful; I think about him climbing that tree.

Since I entered the café, the noise of the crowd has grown louder, the festivities quickened by a touch of frenzy. A table has become available outside, and I sip my glass of wine as I observe the movement around me. The conversation nearby is starting to become disjointed, punctuated by intermittent hysterics. A well-dressed woman at the table next to me is leaning back in her chair, about to doze off; her husband is explaining something to their friend, but keeps losing his train of thought.

Two men in their early twenties are attempting to befriend a group of women at the adjacent table, without much success. There is singing in the air, though the harmonies are now somewhat erratic.

Around twenty minutes later, I sense someone approaching and turn to see Vincenzo coming toward me. He reaches for my empty glass, and as I pass it to him his fingers brush lightly against mine. Everything around us stands still for a few seconds as he lingers, watching me.

"So," he begins in a low voice, that quizzical expression on his face again. He moves his weight from one leg to the other, assuming the mannerisms of shyness, if not the attitude. "My shift finishes in half an hour. Perhaps we could go somewhere and have a drink?"

He seems so certain about the outcome of the evening that for a moment I toy with the idea of storming off, but for some reason I don't. I look down at the table and make a few assessments in quick succession: he is stronger than me, that much is clear, but I can conceal my sharpest knife within reach, just in case; the rest of the village will be too preoccupied with the midnight competition to notice our movements; I like the way I feel when his eyes are locked on mine.

I look back up at him and before I fully know what I'm doing, I nod, almost imperceptibly. His smile widens, the corners of his mouth creasing in a way that fills me with a yearning I have not felt in years.

"*La casa del soldato?*" he asks in a whisper. How does everyone in this village know everything about me, I wonder, before the thought is replaced by more pressing concerns.

"The path that leads into the woods, an hour from now," I find myself murmuring. "Watch out for the Rossettis' dog as you go past the farm." My heart is racing so fast in my chest I feel nauseous. "I'll help you find the way in the dark."

8

In the early hours of the morning, I wake to find him quietly putting on his boots and letting himself out. Light is streaming in through the shutters, particles of dust drifting through the air and reflecting the pale rays of sun. I take a deep breath and notice that I can smell him on me, which sends a fresh wave of pleasure coursing through my body. I close my eyes again and drift in and out of sleep, dreaming strange and sensuous dreams.

I get up close to midday. The sun is too high in the sky for me to go on any walks, and I have no work to be getting on with, so I spend the afternoon reading poetry in bed: Coleridge suits the sultry weather, and my mood. As the sun goes down I sit outside the house, watching the sky turn from cerulean blue to lilac, coral-tinged clouds drifting over the trees, and I breathe in the sweet late-summer air.

The next day, the rain comes. It starts with a smattering of drops, soon becoming quicker and more insistent. I bring in my few gardening tools to stop them from becoming rusty, and put a saucepan on the floor in a corner of the room, where the roof leaks during heavy rainfall. The arid earth outside is replaced by gray swirls of mud; before long, the clearing around the house resembles a shallow lake, silver with the reflection of the sky. I put some wood in the stove, wrap myself in a thick blanket and read about transcendentalism.

*

Over the following months, as the nights grow colder, I go down into the village occasionally, ensuring that I sit at the other café, closest to the town hall; if I see Vincenzo we nod and move on, avoiding all but the most cursory eye contact. I do my best to uphold an image of utmost propriety: I have coffee with the Barbieris, I tutor children in theology, I pay my visit to the priest, donation in hand.

After dark, Vincenzo makes a habit of coming up to see me when his shift is over, bringing a bottle or two that the owner won't miss. Every now and then he disappears for weeks at a time, turning up again with no warning or explanation; I ask none of him. I am under no illusion that I am the only woman whose bed he keeps warm at night, but he doesn't boast about the others, and has never made me feel as though my presence is unwanted.

He raps a specific knock on the door so as not to alarm me, letting me know it's him. We chat about our respective days, and as he opens the first bottle he tells me about the amusing things his customers have said and done since we've last seen each other.

After two glasses of wine, he starts to talk about revolution, which he assumes, correctly, that I will find charming.

After three, he starts to talk about the soldier. "He was a deserter, wasn't he?" he asks the first time the subject comes up.

"Was he?" I reply, genuinely interested. "I don't know anything about him." There were no clues as to his political or philosophical beliefs in the filth he left behind.

"Conscientious objectors, they call it," says Vincenzo, a little drunk. "I do understand why they do it, from an ethical standpoint. But there's nothing conscientious about leaving your fellow soldiers behind. When you sign up, you swear an oath."

I have opinions on this too, but I hold my tongue; I am a woman, and soft-hearted, and my views on the intricacies of war and valor are not what Vincenzo comes here for.

Later, in bed, none of it matters; he is firm and hard and his stubble is rough against my skin. Afterward, pressed up next to him in the cramped space, I am careful not to stir and disrupt his slumber; soon I drift off and sleep through the night.

One day, as a thunderstorm rages outside, he spots my bottle of laudanum, another vice we have in common. We both take a few drops and everything slows down; we spend hours stroking each other, not quite awake. Everything is heightened, exquisite: the quality of our jokes, the colors of the sky, the sensation of his hands on my body.

9

The leaves change color one by one, then seemingly all at once. I have come to know the trees, the fields, the bushes as constant, peaceable companions on my walks; I greet my favorites as I pass, the same yet subtly transfigured since I arrived last autumn. Each plant changes in its own time: one day a branch has lost its flowers, the next, another is adorned with ruby foliage hanging from copper strings. Every day I am greeted with vegetation I have never noticed before, a new configuration of sprigs and fronds that enchants me for a few moments as I pass.

The essence of the light mutates, from a white-hot heat that turns all it touches an etiolated blue, to a warm wash of golden sun deepening the landscape's pigments into those of an oil painting. The sun, and I, rise later now, the race to the top of the pass less frenetic; even at its highest point, the heat of the day is softer on the skin. Once at the top, I rest for as long as my commitments allow before turning back down again, my thoughts quieter, less insistent. From up high I can see no evidence of human life, aside from the occasional cluster of cabins in the distance; the only sounds are those of birdsong, the creaks of the forest. While the days are still mild, I take every opportunity to bathe in the streams I come across, the moss-covered stones viscous and playful underfoot, the water silky and transparent.

Time passes at a magisterial pace some days, when I can't quite believe how many hours are still to come; other times, afternoons disappear in an instant, leaving me disoriented and adrift. The sun sets earlier and earlier, the shadows cast by the surrounding peaks rising up the valley at a speed almost visible to the naked eye. I soon adjust to the changing rhythms; instead of my draconian pocket watch, my movements are regulated by those of the sun, by the particular way darkness starts to fall in the afternoons. My engagements in town become less frequent, so I am freer to adjust my plans to the rapid fluctuations in weather and light, to the whims of my body.

I purchase almanacs and books on the area's flora and fauna; I learn the names and behaviors of insects and birds, unraveling new layers of intricacy in my surroundings. I read about spruces, larches and pines, about poplars, elms, birches and linden trees. In the woods I look out for chamois and marmots, salamanders and frogs; in the sky, I see buzzards and choughs, kestrels and woodpeckers, sparrowhawks and wallcreepers.

I carry a notebook with me in which I jot down what I see—a new plant, an unusual cloud formation, animal tracks—and sketch mammals, birds, nests made from twigs and mud. I log temperatures and measure rainfall in an old jug positioned against a stone in the center of the clearing; I collect leaves and dried flowers, which I press and conserve in a wooden box back at the house. I adapt my habits to interfere less with those of the forest: I take longer routes to steer clear of animals and their young, I avoid brightly colored clothes, I take pains to keep my footsteps silent, fading as much as possible into the undergrowth. Instead of striving always for the summit, I learn to wander without a fixed aim, absorbing the essence of the mountain around me.

Whenever I can, I pay a visit to a tall pine tree, which stands alone in a glade near the top of the pass. Some days its thick trunk and branches appear dazzling, life-giving, a variegated display of greens and browns glistening in the sun; other times, it stands majestic and vast, dark as the night, absorbing particles of color from everything that surrounds it. I brush my fingers along the pine needles, which feel prickly and soft at the same time; I press my palm against the bark, cool and solid like the inside of a cave. Standing in the shade underneath its boughs, I feel protected, enclosed, as though the ancient tree is keeping out all danger. It brings to mind a similar pine in the hills near my aunt's house; children would play hide and seek around it, cowering under its awning, alternating between fearful and thrilled.

One afternoon I get caught in a sudden burst of rain which renders the ground so slippery that walking becomes impossible. After a frantic search I find shelter under an overhanging rock, a dusty den of cobwebs and twigs I can nestle in. Almost immediately I hear a low noise and turn around to glimpse a creature walking ahead of me through the trees. It is gunmetal gray, feral, larger than a dog. Its movements steady and controlled in a way that suggests considerable strength. I hold still, following it with my eyes, and breathe as lightly as I can, not daring to move a finger. I hear nothing, so I stay frozen in the same position, every sense amplified, vigilant. Minutes come and go, and I fall into a daze, watching the rain fall in front of me, thunder rumbling like artillery in the distance. After a while I fall into an uneasy sleep, waking much later to find myself cramped into a ball, aching and stiff. I cautiously look around, but the beast is nowhere to be seen.

The landscape's amber tones fade; a few weeks later, the snow starts to fall, covering the sweep of evergreens in a pristine, powder-blue white. The lake in the valley below appears turquoise, a ghostly mirror that deconstructs its surroundings into shimmering fragments. The cold is so extreme it feels clean, purifying. It stings my eyes and face like invisible daggers, though it is more bearable than the wet autumn days in which the moisture seemed to seep into my bones. My walks become more vigorous, dictated by the need to keep my limbs moving, warm blood running through me. As the weather worsens, my routes become more contained; the risk of sudden blizzards is too great. My world becomes smaller, harsher, and yet ablaze with possibility, slave only to the rules of the mountain.

As the winter roils outside my windows, my cabin becomes a place of refuge from the snow. My thoughts start slowly to placate, little by little; after being in disarray for so long, they begin to coalesce into a shape that is less jagged. Distance, and stillness, allow me to observe the events of the past years with greater clarity: although the pain still feels fresh, I am able to understand it better. I write pages and pages about what I have lost, about the life I will never have. One night I put the pages in the fire, watching each one turn to ashes, as though that could extinguish the memories within. The next day I write a letter, and drop it off at the village post office before I have time to change my mind.

I chop birch and oak for the stove, a neat pile I store in the corner of the room; pine roots, fat with resin, are my kindling. I soon get used to having splinters in my hands, the skin scoured as if by sandpaper, knuckles emblazoned with incisions. I spend whole evenings prying out the slivers by the light of the lamp; I press a paste made from local herbs onto the wounds to avoid infection, and wrap them in gauze overnight. My meals become heartier, more nourishing; I learn what will give me strength over the longest period of time. At night, the wine infuses my body with an inner fire.

Days and weeks pass in a haze, distinguishable only by the changing weather; my perception of dates and months becomes nebulous. A market appears in the village with stalls selling roasted chestnuts, wooden toys, packets of dried mushrooms. Festive decorations bedeck the trees and houses, then vanish. My routine remains the same, a strict and invigorating master; I surrender the agony of choice to the dependability of need. I spend my days and nights alone, for the most part, relieved to leave the world behind.

10

"You should get a dog," says Vincenzo one afternoon, striking a match to light a cigarette as he leans on the windowsill, gazing at the gray skies outside. He looks pale in the harsh mid-winter light, deep shadows under his eyes.

He is right, of course, but I resent the tone he has taken: proprietorial, masquerading as protective. It's a tone I've heard many times in the past, though not from him.

I say nothing, so he turns around, looking at me. "It's not right, you know." He paces around the small room, spilling ash on the ceramic tiles. "You living alone out here. It's dangerous."

"The big bad wolves?" I ask, flatly.

"Wolves, yes—I know you're not being serious, but they kill people in the woods here every year. Lightning, I don't know. What if there's a fire?"

"I'm not sure being in the village would make me burn any slower."

I am being facetious, but I am aware of the dangers. It's not that I haven't thought of them before; I have evaluated the trade-off and made my decision accordingly.

"People in town talk about you," he offers at last. "*Men* talk about you. I've heard them, joking about how you live out here, all alone." He pauses. "Joking about the things they would do to you. I hate it." If I weren't so annoyed, I'd want to comfort him; he appears truly distraught.

"I didn't realize you cared so much what people in town thought," I say, and turn back to the book I'd been reading.

"And I didn't realize you cared so little about what I think. Or about your own safety," he mutters, grabbing his things and pulling the door shut behind him as he leaves. I know he didn't mean it to sound like a threat, but I can't shake a disquieting feeling for the rest of the day.

*

He brings me flowers; we make up. I promise him I'll think about getting a dog. We go for long walks along quiet paths, away from prying eyes. He brings me a small wooden carving of a seabird made by his carpenter friend. We talk about our childhoods.

Then, a few weeks later, seemingly out of nowhere in the middle of dinner, he brings up my husband; another rumor that has made its way into his ear.

"Do you really want to have this conversation?" I ask.

"Yes," he asserts. "I want to know who the woman I'm sleeping with is married to." His nostrils flare slightly as he speaks, something I have never noticed before.

"What do you want to know?"

"His name. What he does. Is it true he's some kind of nobleman?"

I let out a bitter laugh. "There is nothing noble about him. He was an awful man, in the distant past, and I'm never going to see him again." I put my fork down, my body tense. "Look, I don't want to talk about him. I'm here with you now."

We change the subject, but Vincenzo is irritable for the rest of the night. Later I lie awake in bed, now too narrow for us both, unable to sleep until dawn starts to break. The next day, we quarrel again.

*

This time, he does not return for more than a month. At first I am furious with him, filled with an ugly, acrid hate that surprises me; I don't sleep, I barely eat, I can't focus on anything I read. The ferocity of the feeling dissipates after a few days, and is soon replaced by a gentle longing which sharpens until I am sick with regret. I start to dream about him, and when I wake I feel certain that he is about to walk in through the door, as if I could will him into returning with the intensity of my thoughts.

There is something so undignified about this state, veering wildly between anguish, fury and self-condemnation as I used to do in my youth, when I would excoriate myself and my actions with a cruel, insistent clarity. And yet part of me furtively regards these extremes of emotion as a tonic, an abrupt end to the amorphous numbness that had engulfed me for the best part of a decade. This feeling of loss, keen though it is, contains both pain and pleasure.

I go over each argument in my head a hundred times, trying to get to the bottom of why these issues caused us to disagree so vehemently; he was not, after all, being unreasonable. I conclude, as I am wont to do, that it is I who is in the wrong, that it is my misbehavior that is causing the rupture, that it is I who must capitulate. But I can see no solution; we both know that our arrangement is only possible because it is secluded from the world. I had been naive enough to hope that things could continue as they had been, day-to-day. But no matter what you do to keep them at bay, the past and the future have a way of closing in, of constricting the air out of the present moment.

11

I watch the clock, encased in its smooth cherry casket, as the minute hand finally clicks into place: midday. It rings twelve times and I shudder at its doleful tones, a sonorous clang that sounds like church. Today, though, it denotes freedom.

"You heard the bell," I say. "Time to clear away your books."

Enrico and Alberto pretend to fall onto the table, marionettes released from above. They emit a series of groans, a display they repeat at the end of every lesson and which invariably continues to amuse them. While their dedication to this joke is superior to any they exhibit toward the contents of the class, I admire the tenacity.

"Very funny," I laugh, not insincerely. "But next time I expect all the biology homework to be completed—no excuses." I ruffle the hair of the youngest, Alberto, whose head remains prostrated in front of him. Meanwhile, Enrico has disappeared from the room without tidying the desk, so I begin to pick up pencils and loose papers.

"Oh, leave it," I turn to find Mrs Barbieri leaning on the doorway, watery eyes emerging from a face like a startled owl. "I'll make them do it later, otherwise they'll never learn." Her voice is high but quiet, a resigned semi-whisper. A cream-collared olive dress encloses her throat, a row of pearly buttons running from chin to waist.

"Thank you," I smile, and reach down to pick up my bag.

"Won't you stop for a coffee?" She tilts her head to one side, sparrow-like now.

"Of course." I know it's code for the exchanging of my stipend in the kitchen, and an excuse to demonstrate her complicated new coffee-maker.

"Bye, Alberto. See you next time."

"Bye, signora Mantovani." He jumps up to give me a timid hug, then runs after his brother. The table now appears even more chaotic, the sole point in the fastidiously taupe room to contain dashes of red and blue and yellow, heaped together at incongruent angles. Thick-framed windows peer through from behind unyielding curtains, a suggestion of sky just visible above the roofs outside. Porcelain knick-knacks, white and gold, beam at me from every available surface: small dogs, piglets, farmers entwined mid-dance with crooked smiles and dots for eyes. A shudder passes through me, as though from a draft; for a second, my skin feels like ice.

I am glad to leave the sitting room behind for the corridor, a cool and calm oasis, until we enter the kitchen, suffused with the aroma of cauliflower boiling on the stove. "Are you sure you can't stay for lunch?" inquires Mrs Barbieri, a necessary charade.

"No, really," I demur. "That's so kind of you to offer but I've got an appointment in town." An unconvincing performance, I admit, but hopefully sufficient for the intended purpose.

She blinks at me several times, as if assessing the plausibility of my excuse. After a moment—and a soft "Ah!"—she turns her attention to the coffee. I sit at the table, perched as lightly on the edge of a chair as I can.

While the children have given up on the initial volley of impertinent questions about my life, their mother continues to attempt new ways of inveigling me to disclose personal details. "I really don't know how you manage," she begins, solicitude itself. "Up there in the woods. Especially in the winter."

The kitchen maid busies herself with lunch preparations, looking warily on as the lady of the house struggles with the coffee-maker, a task she is intent on completing unassisted.

Mrs Barbieri fills the bottom half of the metal pot with water, then adds ground coffee to the filter, covering the counter with a generous sprinkle of dark powder in the process. She combines the two containers, then fits on the top half of the pot and positions the contraption onto the heat.

"It's perfectly fine," I assure her. "It's only a small room, so it's easy to keep warm. And there's plenty of wood around to put in the stove." I don't go into how exactly the wood gets chopped, to spare her the mental image of me wielding an axe.

She gazes down at the coffee pot, cooing with concern. "Honestly, my dear," she says, gazing into my eyes. "If there's anything we can do, will you let us know?" She stands up straight, remembering who she is. "I know my husband would be more than happy to help."

The coffee has taken on a distinctly burned smell, so she frowns at it for a minute until a thin trickle of steam starts to rise from a hole in the side of the machine. "There we go," she exclaims. The final step, seemingly her favorite, is picking up the whole thing with an oven mitt and turning it upside down, which she achieves with aplomb. "*Ecco fatto!*" she cries, triumphant.

As the water percolates, she excuses herself from the room and goes to find her purse. I hear fumbling, then knocking, and then the sound of a muted conversation through the wall. The maid and I smile at each other, the cauliflower and charred coffee mingling potently in the air. For a second it looks like she might be about to say something, then thinks better of it.

After another minute, the Barbieris surface together from the corridor, the husband bearing a brown leather wallet.

"How are you today, signora Mantovani," he booms, reaching out a large hand, which feels warm and clammy as I shake it. Behind him his wife is arranging the coffee cups, which clink in their saucers as she pours the murky liquid.

"Not too bad, thank you. Enrico and Alberto are making great progress in their work," I half-lie.

"That's good to hear." His expressive eyebrows do a little dance over his sad, friendly eyes. He reaches into his wallet to rifle through some bills. "Thank you for all you're doing for them." He passes me the money, then clasps my hands in his. "If there's *anything* we can do," he adds, his wife's words echoing in his like a shadow. "We'd love to help."

*

Later that day, I feel on edge. I have an early dinner, polenta with foraged mushrooms, and add a few pieces of wood to the stove. It's a drizzly, dismal evening, a forceful wind whistling outside, spattering drops of rain onto the windows. I stuff a blanket along the bottom of the door in an attempt to keep the air out, but sharp blasts creep in from unseen crevices.

At one point I think I hear something unusual, so I get up and look outside the window. I have recently come to regard the bushes and trees that surround the house with some suspicion: while I haven't seen anything out of the ordinary, I am convinced I have heard things—footsteps, branches creaking in an unsettling way. Could there really be men lurking in the shadows there? I think about the Barbieris' concern, about what Vincenzo told me. I try to imagine the things that have been said about me in town; after I have come up with a few possibilities, I try to forget them.

Once I've finished the meal, I wash the plates and pans and go over my diaries from the day, in which I had been making notes about leaf patterns. I start to shiver, a feeling of cold coming over me despite the heat from the stove. I add a bit more wood and watch it burn, entranced by the dancing orange glow enveloping the logs. My shivering intensifies, and as I stand up I realize I am dizzy. I wrap myself in a coat and huddle on the bed; my mind feels torpid, lost in impenetrable fog.

I long for Vincenzo's touch, his warm body, his gentle teasing. His visits are rarer now; we have stopped arguing, but there is less joy in our encounters. The last few times he has come by have been late at night, usually after he has been drinking; once he was so inebriated I turned him away. In any case, tonight it is too early for him to appear at my doorstep; his shift won't end for hours.

My eyes feel like they're burning, and a wave of fatigue washes over me. I set about changing into my nightclothes but find I don't have the energy to do so: no matter, my day clothes feel cocoon-like, so I wrap them tighter around my body. I put out the light, lie down on the bed and close my eyes.

I drift in and out of sleep, dreaming about the beach. I am at my parents' house, although it isn't quite, and I can hear seagulls squawking. I go out of the front door and instead of the usual patio I find that I'm back in my primary school, its dilapidated classrooms eerily empty. I step outside and hear birds all around, though none whose call I can identify. I walk past the sports ground and find myself drawn to the forbidden enclosure at the back, where children used to claim they had seen a statue of the Madonna weeping blood. As I approach, I peer through the trees; I can just about see a shape starting to materialize when I hear a loud crack that startles me awake.

My heartbeat is hard and irregular as I sit up; my body crawls with something corrosive, as if my blood has been replaced by acid. I look to the door, and then at the fire crackling in the corner. I peer through the gaps in the shutter closest to me, not making a sound; I can see only trees in the dim light. My breath feels shallow, insufficient. I try to get back to sleep, telling myself it was probably a log in the fire. But, just as I place my head on the pillow, there it is, again—a brisk, delicate knock, incontrovertibly human, coming from the door.

I'm wide awake now. It is different from Vincenzo's knock; even at his drunkest, he has not deviated. I stand up as quietly as possible and tiptoe toward the kitchen, where I retrieve my biggest knife and grip it hard in my fist.

I step back and take a deep breath. "Who's there?" I ask, hoarse, terrified. I feel like I might faint.

For a second, nothing. And then, a voice from the darkness.

"Laura? Laura, is that you?"

I recognize it at once.

"It's me," I croak, putting down the knife. I unlock the door and look out into the shadows. "Héloïse?"

II

1

I breathe in the air: in it there is salt, might, power. The wind buffets me so that I almost lose my balance, but I keep my eyes shut. I grip the lean iron railing in front of me to steady myself, standing firm and heavy. The smell is almost the same, I think, although I know I don't truly believe it.

Once I open my eyes, the contrast is even more apparent. The sea of my youth was a gentle one: soft, sandy beaches, wide and long; a shallow seabed on which you must pass bank after bank to get to deep water; the colors alternating between olive green and translucent emerald; the occasional pinch of a crab. But this is another kind of sea: inhospitable, wild, the bright hard sun clashing with the waves' violent blues. Even the wind is different; sharper, somehow, more alive. Toward the horizon, the reflections start to dissolve, a dusting of broken crystal; sea and sky fuse together, so that the boundary between them is impossible to distinguish.

Another drawn-out breath and I take a few steps back, resting against the rock wall. It will soon be time for lunch, when my presence will be required, but I linger another minute, taking in the rapidly changing colors out to sea, a scattering of fishing boats emerging from a seemingly endless expanse of water. Around me, the path is bare. Succulents and ashen shrubs cling to the cliffs; sun, wind and sea have cleaved away all but the hardiest forms of vegetation. All surfaces I touch feel scalding, as though they have absorbed hundreds of years of sunlight, ready to sting any intruder who comes too close.

As I turn back on myself the final stretch of path comes into view, patches of grass and flowers sprouting among the stones. I squint in the sunlight and locate the white, two-story house that will be my home for the summer, just visible above the greenery. Between here and there, a handful of people: I steel myself for the encounter, uncrumpling my face from the frown that formed on it while I wasn't paying attention.

"Madame," says a man in his sixties, a flash of bald patch as he tips his hat.

"Bonjour," I trill, relieved that his face is an unfamiliar one. I speed along the footpath, hunger quickening my step. Purple bursts of bougainvillea line the walls, palm trees casting paltry specks of shade as I leave behind the openness of the promontory. Fifteen minutes later I am climbing up the secluded pathway that leads to the house, a lattice of branches providing respite from the midday sun. I unlock the gate and approach the back door; muffled voices come from inside, the melodic cascade of a woman's laughter.

I knock on the kitchen door and let myself in, greeting Marie as she slices radishes on a wooden board, then turn to Pierre, who is resting his heavy elbows on the scuffed table in the middle of the room.

"It's such a beautiful day," I say breathlessly, and Pierre scoffs.

"Wind's coming from inland," he shakes his head. "It's too muggy for me. Bad for fishing, too. Last week the weather was perfect, you should have seen it: fresh air from the sea, clear blue skies. Fantastic for the plants."

"I can imagine," I smile, only now becoming aware of a stuffiness in the air. "It still feels like heaven compared to Paris—it's the first time I've seen the sun in weeks." They both look horrified.

"You couldn't pay me to live there," states Marie solemnly. "I spent a winter up north and my knee ached every time it rained—every day, for six months."

"I can understand that—I'd much rather live here too," I say, and realize I mean it. Glimpses of Paris fulminate in my mind. I try to set them aside. "Is there anything I can do to help with lunch?"

"Absolutely not," she replies, becoming animated. "It will be ready in ten minutes."

"Whenever you're ready," I assure her. I get the feeling that without Julien around they don't take me entirely seriously, so I try to disappear into the background as much as I can, careful not to disturb their established routines.

I get changed upstairs, and when I descend I find my lunch ready on the veranda; a zucchini and goat's cheese tart and a crisp green salad. Marie and Pierre have retired to their rooms for coffee, the aroma of which drifts agreeably through the house. The garden looks peaceful: an olive tree dominates the back corner; along the side, a carefully tended vegetable patch; across the lawn, a jumble of roses, sunflowers, buddleia, hibiscus. While the sea is not visible from here, its presence infuses everything around: seagulls slice through the sky and the air is languid with enforced slowness.

I think again about the conversation in the kitchen: perhaps Julien could be convinced to allow me to stay for the autumn. But when I picture his response the answer becomes apparent; I suppress a cold blast of laughter threatening to rise up, hard and insincere in my throat. I finish my salad and light a cigarette, overlooking the smooth sway of the leaves as the breeze passes through them. After lunch I head to my room and unpack a few more of the clothes I've brought with me, then lie on the bed and read for five minutes before drifting into a serene sleep.

*

By the time I wake up the light has changed again, falling through the foliage and onto the terracotta tiles with a flickering chiaroscuro effect. The sea, which I can see from my window above the trees, looks darker now, less disciplined. I feel drowsy yet refreshed, letting my fingers brush the rough wall as I walk downstairs, partly to steady myself, partly for the sheer tactile pleasure it brings. I hear voices again, this time more of them, and as I advance toward the kitchen I realize who the additional guest is.

"Antoine?" I say, peeking around the door.

"Ma chère!" He looks up at me and grins, cigarette dangling under his thin moustache. He is sitting at the table opposite Pierre and Marie, all three clutching a handful of playing cards with stubborn determination. "I would get up and say hello but, as you can see, I am engaged in a matter of the utmost importance."

"I can see that. Who's winning, then?"

"Well, that would be telling," Antoine responds, brow furrowed.

"Not this one, that's for sure," interjects Pierre before erupting into a cackle. "Your turn, monsieur."

"We'll see about that," Antoine protests, eyes darting at his competitor. After some dithering, he plucks two cards from his selection and places them slyly on the table.

Pierre and Marie burst out laughing. "Next time we play for money," she chortles, placing down two of her own before picking up the central pile. The men lay down their cards and applaud slow and begrudging claps.

Antoine stubs out his cigarette and rises to greet me, a peck on each cheek. "Won't you join us for a game?"

"I'd better not inflict my card-playing on anyone. And by the looks of it neither should you."

"Ha ha. I'll have you know, I was doing brilliantly until you walked in."

"Right then," declares Marie. "Everyone out of here. I've got to start shelling peas for tonight."

We disperse; Pierre to the front of the house, where he is putting together a wooden fence, while Antoine and I make our way to the garden with a bottle of wine. He folds his tall, lithe body onto a chair next to the cast iron table, the seat protected by an embroidered cushion. Everything looks perfect, resplendent in the afternoon sun.

"Monstrous, as always," he muses, taking in the surroundings with a wry smile.

"Frightful. When did you get here, then?" I start pouring the wine.

"Yesterday afternoon." His eyes narrow, a sure sign he has something interesting to say.

"Are you staying with the same friend as last year?"

"Oh, him," he wrinkles his nose. "No—that's a long story. I've made a new friend."

"Do tell."

"I met him in Les Halles a month or so ago. Works in a bank, but don't hold that against him. Old, but not too old—good-looking in a distinguished kind of way. Never married, which makes things easier."

"He sounds wonderful. What's his name?"

"Claude. You'd like him. You both hate Paris. And chardonnay."

"Can't wait to meet him. Whereabouts is his place?"

"Not far—in the hills near Villefranche."

"Lucky you." We clink glasses.

When we are reaching the end of the bottle, Antoine looks at me, then says in a quiet voice, "When is he arriving?"

My throat tightens. "Tomorrow," I manage to say.

We watch the olive tree swaying in the wind; a chicken walks into view across the lawn, its head flitting erratically to the ground and back.

"Darling," says Antoine gently. "I know it's been a difficult few months. If there's anything we can—"

"I'm fine," I assert, my voice frostier than I had intended. "Really," I adjust my tone to one I hope he will find conciliatory. "We just need some time by the seaside. I'm sure we can work things out."

I can feel his eyes on me as I stare at my hands. "I'm sure you will," he agrees, his voice soft.

We sit in silence as the chicken continues its aimless search, neck jerking up and down like an involuntary spasm.

2

The next morning, I'm out of bed at first light and set about my routine with alacrity. I bathe, the water as close to scalding as I can bear, my skin softening and shriveling like a raisin infused in rum. I massage the ends of my hair with fragrant oil and wrap each strand into a tightly wound curl, which I fasten to my scalp and allow to dry. In the meantime, I apply depilatory cream to my upper lip, arms and legs; it tingles on my freshly scoured flesh, a sensation I never fail to find oddly gratifying. Once the necessary time has elapsed, I wipe everything off with a cloth, coarse hairs mingling with lotion like flecks of dirt on snow. I lather ointment onto my body and rosewater on my face, followed by a rich moisturizing cream and a dusting of powder. For now, I put on a simple cotton day dress, which hangs airy and loose around my oiled limbs.

Downstairs, preparations are in full flow: surfaces shine like new, floor tiles polished into a glistening dampness, laundry fluttering outside. A whir of activity comes from the kitchen, but the conversation now is muted, focused.

"Morning, madame," says Marie, balancing a stack of plates from one side of the room to the other. "I've left your breakfast outside. I'm just about to head to the market—is there anything in particular you want for tonight?"

"Good morning," I reply, moving out of her way. "Yes—thank you. I've written out a list here—" I place a folded sheet of paper on the table "—I was thinking we could have grilled sea bass with new potatoes, asparagus and lemon." I do my best to sound authoritative, a demeanor that does not come naturally to me. "And make sure you get the fish from Fabrice's stall—Julien always complains if we get it anywhere else."

"Naturally," says Marie. Relieved of her load, she picks up the list and inspects it, nodding. *"Pas de problème."*

"Thank you." I feel tense, alert, like everything is moving slightly too fast. "Pierre, has the back door been fixed? It was creaking again yesterday." The tone sits uneasily on my lips; I feel queasy.

"That's my next job," he explains, patiently. "But first I've got to paint the fence, so that it will be dry in time." For the moment, he is finishing a cigarette at a leisurely pace at odds with the bustle around him, but I have neither the wish nor the wherewithal to hasten him along any more than I already have.

I sit down to breakfast: black coffee, orange juice, a slice of bread smeared with butter and marmalade. My nausea turns out to be hunger; I check the time and realize I have been awake for hours. I devour the food in a few bites, drain the coffee and juice. I wish for more but I stop myself, aware that any excesses in my appetite will not go unnoticed. My mind scans the house, the refreshments, my body for possible faults that might be cause for grievance. There is still much to be done.

Hours pass in near-silence. Everyone loses themselves in their tasks as if in a reverie: plates are polished, clothes ironed, carpets beaten. Chaos is turned step by step into a veneer of order. Once the heat of the day has become less blistering, I change into an elegant but understated satin gown. My hair has dried into soft waves, which I style into a look dictated by my husband's taste. I finely line my eyes and eyebrows, and apply the faintest trace of rouge to my cheeks and lips. My movements are methodical, precise; my reflection stares back at me, features accentuated as though by delirium or desire, my expression impassive.

After the day's drudgery, the house is pristine, the air rich with the scent of butter and sliced vegetables. The dining room has been set, with Pierre adding the finishing touches: a vase of flowers, candles ready to be lit. He has changed from his open-chested calico shirt into a stiff high-collared garment.

"Evening," he says, in a somber voice. "I'll be heading down to the station shortly. The train from Paris arrives at six forty-seven, is that correct?"

"That's the one," I nod. "Thank you, Pierre."

In the kitchen, Marie is dressed up under her apron, hair immaculate despite the flurry of steam and saucepans around her.

"Everything looks wonderful," I say, and she beams at me. Around her, the food has been carved and assembled, ready for the final steps.

While we wait, Marie disappears into her room and I pick up a bottle from the wine cooler. I sit on the veranda, drinking steadily; I have a book with me, but I keep reading the same page. The wine makes me giddy, then bold, fortified against what the evening will bring. I am mindful of not exceeding a certain limit; over the years, I have perfected the art of finding the exact point at which inebriation becomes palpable.

At seven o'clock, Marie goes back to the kitchen and starts chopping herbs and lemons. I go upstairs to peer out from the window at the end of the corridor, which faces the path below. It is difficult to see through the leaves and shadows, but I can discern no human form. I check my reflection again, compulsively inspecting each flaw. I blot the oil from my forehead, apply more powder. I sit on the bed, keeping a foot on the ground to steady myself after the wine. I drink some water and let a eucalyptus lozenge dissolve in my mouth.

After half an hour, I look out of the window again; nothing. I go down to check on Marie, who is pacing up and down the dining room.

"Do you think something has happened to Pierre?" she asks, trying to mask the worry in her voice.

"I'm sure Pierre is fine. The train has probably been delayed," I assure her. "It happens all the time." I have another glass of wine.

At eight o'clock, nothing has changed. I sit on the veranda again, watching the sky change from gold to red to blue.

After another hour has passed, I go back inside. "What if he's had an accident?" Marie's concern is now unmistakable. "This isn't like him." I open my mouth to console her, but no words come out. My thoughts are filled with locomotives overrunning their tracks, of metal crashing into soft tissue; images I regard with no particular emotion.

Eventually, a light becomes visible on the path below. I strain my eyes in the gloaming, but I can't make out if it is one person or two. I go back downstairs, and Marie and I stand outside the front door.

The light gets closer, and she walks over to open the gate. I see from a distance that it is Pierre; she embraces him, still shaking, while he tenderly squeezes her shoulder. They talk in hushed tones for a while, Marie appearing to admonish him for his delay. Then they turn to me, and start to walk in my direction.

I steel myself as they reach me. Pierre doesn't know where to look.

"I'm sorry." He holds his hat in his hands. "He wasn't on the train. I waited for the nine fifteen from Paris, and he wasn't on that one either."

We stand in silence for a moment.

"Was it definitely today that he was coming?" Marie hazards, in a small voice.

I regain my composure. "Yes—I checked the letter several times." I look at Pierre. "And he didn't send a telegram?"

They exchange a glance. "Er—no," he replies, eyes to the ground. "No telegram."

I feel exhausted, the air crushed from my lungs.

"I can still cook dinner," offers Marie. "It would be a shame to waste that nice fish."

"You two have it. I'm going to bed." I am too tired for niceties; I need to be alone.

As I leave, they gaze at me with something approaching pity, and I am repelled by the image of me they see. I think of Julien and am filled with a venomous and overpowering hatred. The humiliation I am used to; if anything, his continued absence is a respite. As I scrub the makeup from my skin in front of the mirror, I do not wonder about his whereabouts, about the poorly formulated excuses he will inevitably provide; it makes no difference to me.

It is only later, when I'm lying in bed listening to the sound of the wind, that I allow my thoughts to return to those visions of carnage and destruction. I turn my head into my pillow and weep and weep, recalling the disappointment I felt when they turned out to be only fantasies.

3

I wake up late the following morning. The prospect of repeating the previous day's errands fills me with a grinding numbness, so my preparations are perfunctory and imprecise, a minimal addendum to the groundwork laid yesterday. I arrange my hair into a sleek bun and wear the same simple cotton dress as the day before.

When I descend, Pierre and Marie eye me with sympathy, so I make a point of displaying my cheerfulness. In truth, I am elated. I let myself imagine the summer ahead, how it might unfold in his absence. The past few days have given me a taste for the solitude I had once enjoyed as a child, a glimpse of life beyond the claustrophobia of Paris.

But Marie looks agitated. "I went to Fabrice's this morning," she starts, "and they were out of sea bass. I didn't know what to do, so I bought sea bream instead. I hope that's all right. I've also bought sea bass from the place around the corner, in case you'd prefer me to cook that tonight. If..." Her voice trails off.

"You've done perfectly, Marie," I tell her. "He might not turn up today at all—he did mention he might be at a conference this weekend," I lie. They both appear relieved by the flimsy excuse.

"I'm going for a walk," I say. "I'll be back in an hour or two."

Outside, I breathe in deeply, detecting that salt again. I try to avoid thinking about the day ahead, what might happen, what might not. The sky is overcast but luminous, the sea a lustrous gray; the air is fresh and invigorating. I walk past a family I recognize from previous years, and we pass each other with a nod.

Their presence feels comforting, providing a sense of continuity without the need for enforced intimacy.

I start to feel hungry so I turn toward town, passing unruly market stalls on the way to the bakery. The shop is bustling, and I position myself in the line, studying the assortment of cakes and quiches on display like jewels. When my turn comes I order a tomato tarte tatin, the small red orbs caramelized and golden, oil already beginning to ooze through the paper bag as they hand it over to me across the counter. I settle up and turn around, and find myself face to face with Madeleine and Anatole Blanchard.

"Madeleine!" I exclaim as her pointed blond features close in, greeting me with a kiss, then another. "Anatole," I add, and repeat the performance.

"*So* good to see you," she smiles coyly. "I love this dress—very rustic."

"Lovely to see you too," I simper back, nails digging into the top of my bag. "It's been so long."

"Is Julien around?" asks Anatole, a dull glint in his eyes.

"Um, not at the moment." I hadn't planned for this. "He's—very busy with work."

"Oh really?" he frowns in confusion. "I could have sworn he said he was coming down this weekend." My stomach clenches into knots.

"I—" I start, but Anatole's revelation is ricocheting through my mind.

Madeleine smirks, shooting him a look. "I'm sure Anatole has it wrong," she dives in, delighted to have saved me from embarrassment.

"Anyway," I say, disentangling myself from the crowd and toward the door. "I better let you get on with your shopping. See you around."

I stumble back outside, my elation from earlier dissipating fast. I hurry back along the seaside path, stopping under the shade of a tree to eat a few bites of the tarte tatin. I can't finish it, so I break it up and throw the pieces to some seagulls which have assembled around me. I hope the family I saw earlier doesn't walk past now.

I walk to the edge of the water and rinse my hands in the waves lapping at the pebbles. I dab a few drops onto my wrists and temples and look out at sea for a minute, the salt crystalizing on my skin, before turning back home.

As I approach the gate, the house appears still, silent. I step into the kitchen and peer into the hallway; at the other end of it, Marie is mending something, a curtain perhaps, at a seat by the window. When she spots me she jumps, then puts a finger to her lips and points toward the study upstairs. I nod.

I tiptoe up the steps, barely breathing. The stairs creak as I climb and my eyes are fixed on the door of the study, which remains closed; reaching the landing feels like the top of a mountain. A couple more steps and I'm in my room, where I softly pull the door closed behind me. I get undressed, dampen a cloth to wipe my face and body, spray on some perfume. I pick out a cream-colored linen dress and a gold and opal necklace he bought me years ago, along with matching earrings. I shake out my hair and brush it with vigor before attempting to recreate the previous day's style.

I am dabbing on a light layer of rouge when I hear movement. I freeze. Two doors down, someone is walking around in the study, prowling. I put away my brushes and arrange myself into the seat overlooking the view, picking up the closest book and turning to an arbitrary page. The door of the study screeches open and I hear steps on the landing, which advance leisurely until they pause just outside my room. A polite rap on the door.

"Are you in there?" His cold baritone.

"I'm here," I reply. I stand, holding my book, as he lets himself in.

To look at him, you would not think him different from any other man. His hair is brown and gray, a high forehead split by deep lines, his slightly too-small eyes neither cruel nor kind. I had thought him good-looking once.

"You didn't think to come in and greet your husband?" His voice is measured, aloof.

"I didn't want to disturb you. I thought you might be resting after your journey." I hold my breath.

A pause. "Very well." He looks me over. "Is that a new dress?"

"I bought it in Paris last month," I tell him, and attempt a smile. I feel bile rising in the back of my throat.

"*C'est bien*," he says without emotion. He turns to go.

"Julien," I start. He faces me again, a touch of irritation in his stance. "At what time would you like dinner tonight?"

He fixes me with his stare, his eyes like slits. His voice is firm. "Eight."

And he is gone.

*

He remains in his study for the rest of the afternoon. The house is quiet: Pierre tends to the vegetable patch, Marie sweeps industriously, I find a shaded corner of the veranda in which to pretend to read. Every noise from upstairs silences us at once; we stand at attention, immobilized while we wait for the door to open.

It stays shut until five minutes to eight, when Julien makes his descent. He has changed into formal evening-wear, as have I: his suit is dark, its severe lines making a clean rectangle of his torso. While we wait for food to be served, he beckons me to join him in the drawing room, where we sit for a second while Pierre approaches.

"Pastis," says Julien. "Lemonade for madame."

"Of course." Pierre bows and withdraws from the room.

I look at my husband, a slight tremor perturbing the corners of my smile. He watches me, as if examining an ornament he deems unsuitable for his mantelpiece.

"So," he begins, impatient with my muteness. "What have you been doing in my absence?"

"Spending time around the house—reading, gardening." This appears to be insufficient, so I continue. "I've been on a few walks along the beach. Oh, I saw Madeleine and Anatole at—"

"Walking alone is not seemly." His face hardens, then, with some effort, he mitigates his expression. "I am thinking only of your character, my sweet." The word sounds like poison in his mouth. "I told Marie this morning—she needs to accompany you in the future."

I look down. "Naturally. I'll make sure of that."

At that moment Pierre arrives, glasses tinkling on a tray. He places them on the table between us, letting us know that dinner will be served shortly.

"You seem well settled here," Julien remarks once Pierre has gone.

"It's beautiful, as always." I try to gauge his demeanor, which appears momentarily sedate. I take my chance, inclining my head toward him in deference. "Actually, I've been wondering if—if I might stay on a little longer in the autumn. Seeing as you've been traveling so much for work."

"While I live in Paris without my wife? We'll talk about this later," he sneers; a flat refusal. I would have thought he'd be glad to be rid of me—I shall try again at the end of the summer.

He sips his drink and we avoid each other's eyes.

"Dinner is served." Marie appears at the door, her voice ringing across the room.

Julien signals for me to go first; I obey. I can't explain why, after all this time, I still feel an obligation to please him. The fear of his reprimands alone, verbal or otherwise, does not account for all of it; part of me is still eager for his approval, if not his affection. His barely veiled contempt exerts a powerful hold over me, evoking a sensation that both electrifies and subdues me.

We take our seats opposite each other at the dining table, which has been laid with a spotless white cloth. Silver candlesticks stand at either side of us; a round vase filled with white flowers is the centerpiece. Pierre pours us both small glasses of white wine as Marie brings through the entrée, scallops on a bed of broad beans.

I wait for Julien to have had a few bites; he seems satisfied, so I ask, "Is everything to your liking?" I consider adding "my love," in the same poisonous tone he used earlier, but I can't quite bring myself to.

He nods, as enthusiastic an answer as I can expect. I watch his jaw's rhythmic movements, the sound of his chewing making my skin shiver. I eat in silence, waiting for him to speak next. But tonight he is not forthcoming, even by his usual standards.

"You saw the Blanchards earlier, you were saying?" He finally relents.

"I did, at the bakery. They seemed well." I do not acknowledge the predicament he put me in. "We'll need to go back there, they do the most amazing—"

"It's *retourner*," he admonishes me, strict as a headmaster. "Not *tourner*. I don't know how many times I've told you."

"I'm sorry. I knew as soon as I said it." I bite the inside of my lip, berating myself.

"Serves me right," he mutters, as if to himself, "for marrying an Italian fishwife."

He holds my gaze, waiting for me to react. An image flashes in my mind of what he had been like when we first met, nearly fifteen years ago; there had been cruelty in his humor, but the kind that could be mistaken for charisma. Now his sharp tongue, which I had once found alluring, has turned its powers against me.

The tension in the room is palpable as Pierre picks up the plates. I have made sure to leave some food on mine: I'll give his sharp tongue nothing more to complain about tonight.

I ignore the taunt; when we are alone again I change the subject, paying particular care to my pronunciation. "What would you like to do tomorrow?"

"I'll be going to Marseilles tomorrow," he announces. "Urgent business." He leans back in his seat, resting his wrists on the table.

"Oh," I say, masking my surprise. I know better than to point out he has only just arrived. "And how long will you be staying?"

"As long as I need to," he replies with a certain relish. The exchange seems to have lifted his spirits; evidently he believes his absence will prove distressing to me.

The next course arrives, and as Pierre is placing the dish in front of Julien I suddenly remember what Marie said about the fish earlier that morning.

"Antoine was here the other day," I say, hoping Julien will be distracted.

"Oh yes?" he says with distaste. "Did you compare ribbons and dresses?"

I feel sick. "We talked about books, mainly. He told me about a play that's on in Nice—we should all go together sometime."

He glares at me, then back down at his plate. He stabs at the fish with his fork and studies it. Then he looks up at me, accusatory. "Pierre—get Marie."

"Julien," I say, serious now. "Leave her out of it—Fabrice was out of sea bass, so I told her this would be all right."

"I'll deal with you later," he spits. He turns to the door, where Marie has appeared, her face pale.

"Monsieur Julien," she begins. "I'm so sorry—"

He shushes her with a soft "tss" sound, and she stares down at her feet. He stands up, towering over her. "Marie, this brings me no pleasure at all. But if you don't listen, you'll never learn."

She nods, blinking moisture from her eyes.

"Now, you know I don't like sea bream. I have told you a million times." His voice is soft now, almost a whisper. "You and your husband get to live in this beautiful house, which belonged to my father, and his father before him, and your only job—" his voice wavers a little "—is to look after the place and keep it in good shape for when we come to stay. And when we come to stay, we want to be treated like *kings*."

"If you please," she mumbles. "I bought sea bass from the place at the top of the market, I can cook it for you now if you—"

"I don't *want* your second choice," he hisses. His voice rises abruptly. "I *want* you to get up at the crack of dawn and make sure you get me the *best* of the—"

"Julien, that's enough." I stand up. "She had it yesterday. We had everything ready for you, exactly how you wanted it, and you didn't even bother turning up."

His head snaps in my direction. "You two, get out," he snarls at the others. They both look at me, and I nod.

When we are alone, we stare at each other until the house has gone quiet. Then he starts to advance in my direction, treading around the table with his fingers trailing its edge.

"If you *dare* ever speak to me like that in front of the servants again—" he skulks up behind me, his breath hot on the back of my neck "—I am going to send you back to the sewer I found you in." He is speaking very quietly, each syllable sharp. "You are nothing without me."

I don't say anything; I know it will only inflame things.

"I pluck you from the dirt, give you my money, give you my name," he murmurs. "And what do I get for it in return, after all these years? *Nothing.* A bad investment—damaged goods." He is in front of me now, a minuscule fleck of spittle clinging to his chin. We both know we're not arguing about the food. "I should have thrown you out years ago."

With that, he is gone. I sit down and take a few deep breaths, glaring at the wall in front of me until my thoughts have dispersed. I am relieved to notice that I do not need to cry, a final indignity I am spared tonight. This kind of display has become so commonplace that I feel almost immune to it; perhaps, one of these days, I will become invulnerable to his whims.

That night I lock the door to my room and lie in bed, careful not to make any noise. I grind my teeth and count the minutes until he is gone from the house; I hate him more than I have ever hated anyone in my life. But, much later, when he raps on my door and demands to be let in, I surrender once more and do as I am told.

4

By the time I wake up he has left for Marseilles. I make my way downstairs, frail and light-headed, and drink a glass of cold water, then another. The previous day has left me husk-like, detached from the world around me. Once I have gathered enough strength I go to Marie's room and knock; she is sitting in a corner, darning a pair of socks. I apologize for my husband's behavior, and attempt to convince her that I am in good spirits. Then I go back to my room, close the shutters and get back into bed.

In the afternoon I have made plans to meet Héloïse in town. I feel ashamed of her seeing me in the state I am in, a thought that brings me to the brink of tears, but I know that if I do not meet her she will suspect something. So I set about my preparations once again, joylessly grooming and preening myself into an approximation of my former self.

The café is flooded with sunlight: curved glass windows reach into the sky, sheer curtains trembling at their side, hanging plants strewn high and low like airborne waterfalls. Outside, the green tops of trees oscillate against the cobalt blue of the sea. I take my seat at a table next to the window and wait for my friend to arrive, keeping my eyes locked on the view.

After a few minutes I hear a rustling behind me, followed by a velvety "Afternoon" as Héloïse's fingertips brush my shoulder. I stand up and we embrace, her body soft and warm against mine; I wish she would never let go.

"It's good to see you." My smile is unforced now, but I worry my eyes will give my agitation away.

"Likewise," she says, taking her seat. "Beautiful view."

I become aware of people at the tables around us darting glances in our direction. Age has done to Héloïse what I had hoped it would do to me: her beauty appears refined by it, the subtle lines around her eyes enhancing her expression rather than distorting it. Her tightly curled hair has been tied back into a graceful chignon, her skin gleams in the sun.

"So how have you been since I last saw you?" I ask, careful not to let the smile slip. "What was it—that endless German opera?"

"Yes—interminable, wasn't it? We should have made a run for it at the interval." She laughs. "I've been fine. Went to visit my mother last week, which was nice but I was ready to leave by the end of it." She looks up at me. "How about you, how have you been?"

I am beginning to put together an answer when the waiter comes to take our order; after a brief discussion, we decide on tea and a slice of lemon sponge cake to share.

"How are the boys?" I ask when he leaves, moving on.

Her face brightens. "They're doing well. Glad to finally be here for the holidays—as am I. It's such a relief to leave everything behind."

"I know what you mean. I wish we never had to go back to Paris," I muse. Héloïse's expression wavers, and I realize I've alarmed her. "Is Eugène here too?" I ask quickly.

"Yes—he's with the boys now. They've gone to the beach to get ice cream."

Before she can turn the question back to me I add, "Antoine came by the other day."

"I know," she says, "we saw him yesterday. We went for dinner together, a new spot he recommended—which was delicious, by the way." Her words are light, but I can tell something is on her mind. She interlocks her fingers in front of her, her face grave. "Laura, is everything all right?"

"I'm fine," I answer as if by instinct, but my tone betrays me. I see the waiter approach with our order and I look down at my hands, which are shaking under the table.

As he walks away, I see Héloïse is cautiously inspecting my throat and arms. "Has he—"

"No," I say, my voice firm. "He's never going to do that again."

"And you take his word for it?" She is annoyed.

"It's how he was brought up. His father was very strict with him." I don't know why I'm defending him. "I think this holiday will do us both a lot of good," I add, aware of how weak this sounds.

Héloïse is watching me with something that might be anger, or concern, or a combination of the two. "I need to talk to you. It's only right you should know."

I've been waiting for this moment, even though I didn't know I was. All of a sudden, I know what she's going to say.

She scans the tables around us, but we are too far from the nearest people for them to hear. Still, she lowers her voice. "You know about his, um—"

I nod. Of course I know.

"—well, she's—she's expecting," she mouths the final word.

I swallow. "I see."

"I was at the theater the other night," Héloïse is now saying, but I can hear only a distant echo of her voice; it's as though my ears are being pressed together, a loud ringing drowning out everything around, "—I was speaking to Adèle—" My thoughts overflow with hordes of faceless figures: I can hear their whispers, their laughter, "—she heard something from her brother—" My breathing has become labored; I thought I was prepared for this, but the ringing, "—it sounds like Julien is going to ask for an annulment."

Everything feels light, unmoored, as though the curtains and plants are spiraling around me; sounds are muffled and distorted.

The sea whirls ceaselessly back and forth, majestic and wild and indifferent.

5

While Pierre and Marie busy themselves downstairs, I rifle through the small pile in the back corner of my wardrobe. All day, careful not to disappear for too long at any one time, I have been assembling a few things, mundane objects that won't be missed: clothes, books, a pair of walking boots, medicine bottles. Earlier this morning, before anyone else was awake, I crept into the study and opened the drawer under the desk where Julien leaves his money, and breathlessly took as many of the larger bills as I dared.

As I formulate my plan, memories come back to me unbidden, a final ploy to make me stay. I have gone through these moments in my mind so many times, to try to recall how I had once felt about my husband, to make sense of how our marriage slowly unraveled. The way the sun would fall on his light brown hair, flecking it with gold; the easy arrogance that was his birthright, so different from the crude behavior of the boys I had grown up with. I had not long turned twenty when I met him, traveling through Italy like some lost Romantic hero. When he brought me home to meet his family he had seemed so cavalier in his disregard for his father's censure, his mother's disapproval of our match. In secret he derided the family name; over dinner tables he proclaimed his love for me as if he were storming the barricades, which in a sense he was. He delighted in parading his shy, low-born wife, an affront to the high society he moved in.

I had thought, at that age, that I knew the ways of the world, that my lowly upbringing had given me an insight into the rough edges of things, into the darker corners that the well-heeled are careful to keep hidden. But I quickly learned how little I knew. Julien took particular pleasure in educating me in the ways of his class, teaching me how to dress, dance and comport myself, which views to hold and how to express them, how my voice ought to sound, how loud I should laugh, so that little by little he had molded me into a creature of his own making. I never thought, in those days, to challenge him: he was like a god to me, my benefactor, even though he did not remind me of such things back then.

The lure of shocking his peers, however, started to fade as he grew older and more inured to the luxurious lifestyle his status ensured. When his father became ill years later, Julien's last vestiges of youthful rebellion fell away, revealing him to be rather more similar to his parents than either of us had imagined. His views on matters of politics and religion changed practically overnight, but this time I was less malleable to his commands, and did not follow as readily where he led. After five years passed, then ten, and it gradually became clear that his once-hated family name would not be continued, he finally started to resent his choice of bride, so that soon it would spite him as much as it had his father before him. Now, when we venture out for social occasions, he conspicuously sits as far from me as possible, sitting close to elegant women of his own rank as though I weren't there, their fingers sympathetically brushing his forearms.

I have known for a long time that this day would come. I have been making a plan, unbeknownst even to myself—in the back of my mind I have it all mapped out. Years ago, I read an article in a newspaper that has stayed with me ever since: a man had killed and buried his wife, hoping to marry his mistress, but the judge had ruled twelve months needed to pass after the spouse's disappearance for the marriage to be annulled on the grounds of desertion; eleven months in, a farmer found the wife's body in a field and the husband was executed for her murder.

I do not suspect Julien of plotting anything quite so brutal, but he has friends in high places, and it is not beyond the realms of possibility that he could have me admitted to an institution of some description. One particular detail of the story has stuck in my mind: perhaps if I can disappear for twelve months I can delay the nuptials, and in so doing deprive him of the heir he so desperately wants. It's possible that in time he will formally adopt the child or have more later in the marriage, but it is pleasing to know just how much the scandal will gall him and his family, and sully that revered name.

When I meet Antoine and Héloïse at the beach, the plan is almost fully formed in my mind, meager and inadequate though it is. The sun is setting and birds circle overhead as though searching for carrion; it is an unseasonably cool night and we are alone on the rocks apart from a few lone swimmers in the distance.

We embrace with a sense of urgency, for a long time. We sit down close to each other, so that we can hear over the sound of the wind and waves, of the seagulls calling overhead.

"I need to get away," I say in a low voice. "I don't want to leave you, or my life here, but I have to go—for a year, at least, maybe longer." I tell them the story from the newspaper. "Next Tuesday, Pierre and Marie will be out of the house—they have the afternoon off and are going inland to visit relatives. I will pack my things, then I need somewhere to stay for a few hours until nightfall. At five past eleven, I'll board the overnight train to Italy at the next station from here."

"You can stay at Claude's," says Antoine, after thinking for a few seconds. "Julien doesn't know where he lives. We're not far from the station."

I nod; I try to say something but my throat is thick with emotion. He puts a hand on mine.

"But where will you go in Italy?" asks Héloïse. "Do you have any family left? Friends?"

I shake my head. "I have to go somewhere where he won't find me, so I don't know precisely where I'm going yet. I won't be able to write to you at first. But I'll let you know where I am once it's safe to do so."

The wind has picked up, so we lean in closer.

"It will be a new start," I say, forcing a smile. "This is what I need to do."

The sun disappears behind the rocks; a translucent orange light falls diagonally across the sky, as though the air were made of lava. Above us, the gulls fly in ever smaller circles, their dissonant calls dispersing in the dusk.

INTERLUDE

At first she sees only colors: a fuzzy succession of greens and reds and purples dancing together on the back of her eyelids, forming into one shape then another like fireworks or trails of slime left behind by snails on a window. She tries to follow them with her pupils, left, right, up, right, left, down, up, but for some reason they do not move, as if they were etched into her mind itself, disconnected from her vision. There are many kinds: small dots, clusters of light, a diffuse backdrop of blue, a monstrous red shape, flashes of gold. She looks from one to the other, a child watching the night sky, and when her eyes tire of moving she lets herself become still, a smudge of pure white light shining at the corner of her eye, overpowering her senses and guiding her to sleep. In her dreams the lights follow her, left, right, down, left, she scrambles to keep up and floats inside them, made of light herself, and everything feels free and loose and her being expands in all directions and then she realizes she is awake again, in between worlds, and she watches the colors shift and mutate until she drifts back into darkness.

*

Liquid is coming out of her lips, eyes, nostrils, every part of her; her limbs are on fire, an acerbic taste in her mouth, acid seeping through her every pore. She is not herself but a vessel, a body repelling an intruder. Her sinews and blood are in charge now, preserving her strength for the next violent retch, then sleep, then again nausea and purgation; she is there, but not there— pure instinct, nebulous and atavistic. Every cell in her body feels inflamed, burning from the inside in a blaze of bewilderment and exhaustion. One second her teeth chatter with cold like she will never be warm again; minutes later she is ripping the bed sheets off like they are made of flames. The pain is constant but its shape and quality change swiftly, attacking first one part of her then another, finding new and insidious ways of surprising her with its malice. Any movement is onerous, tissues creaking against their will, but staying still is torment: insistent aches, an overwhelming dullness, a chilling taste of oblivion. Her heartbeat feels too fast, too thick, too hard, too much. For every second she's awake she longs for release; anything to make it stop.

*

Shapes move above her and she watches the shadows play on the ceiling, her eyes fluttering open and shut. She thinks she knows where she is, but after she wakes her dreams linger insistently in her mind, so that half of her remains in the places she left a moment ago, angular simulacra of half-remembered buildings in which invisible and unknown dangers lurk.

*

After she doesn't know how long, a day, a week, impossible to tell, she becomes aware of a voice softly singing in the corner. She stays still, like a rock; maybe it has not seen her. She continues with her ingenious stratagem, not making a sound, her stillness rendering her body invisible, until the singing leaves the room and she is safe once again.

*

She sniffs the air, and through her mucous membranes the aroma of something edible starts to percolate. Her head twitches in the direction of the smell, which battles with her nausea and, after some tussle, emerges as the victor. She sees a shadow move and by now she is certain she is not alone, so she attempts her immobilization trick once again but finds, to her horror, that the shape is coming closer, and closer, not fooled by her at all, and it is near her now, their two forms joined in the penumbra of the ceiling, and the shape is opening her mouth, which she clamps shut, but it is holding her head now, the warm metal of a spoon prying open her lips and she spits out the poison, but it's not poison, it is soup, its salt and warmth penetrating her tongue so she opens her mouth for more.

*

The outhouse, these days, is a distant and impossible chimera; she relieves herself in the pot the shape has left for her, shielding herself with a mantle of shame.

*

The figure gradually takes shape; from shadow to outline to head hovering over her like a balloon. She does not like it, but she needs it, and accepts its ministrations with goodwill. She finds that its singing has become pleasing to her, and she awaits its food with increasing voracity, so that she begins to salivate as soon as the clanks of metal and wood begin their regular concerto from the corner of the room.

*

She sleeps for more than a day, or for only a second; when she wakes, the light outside is exactly the same. In her dreams she is flying: she floats just above the pine trees, brushing their tips as she goes. She flies up and up, past streams and plains and rock faces and lakes, until she's in the middle of the sky, as high as the jagged mountaintops dusted in snow, the moon shining down on the corrie below, everything shimmering and blue. She is free of weight, of pain; she is the air, the river, the mountain, and at that moment she realizes she is in a dream and cries out, because she knows that dreams cannot survive self-awareness, not for long, not truly, and while she grasps for this feeling to continue she starts to fall, her attempts to hold on warping the energy into something else entirely as she plunges through the night until she lands with a *thud*, and she is awake.

III

1

Everything is blurry at first, but I recognize my room at once, its configuration of wooden furniture on off-white walls. I try to sit up but I am too weak, so I wait for the dizziness to pass. I feel a globule of phlegm clinging to the back of my throat, so thick I can hardly breathe. I look around and see that someone has left a clean handkerchief beside my bed, so I reach out and clear my throat into it, carefully enfolding the contents like a gift. The air is reaching my lungs now, and I have awakened enough to get up onto my elbows and take in my surroundings; I wonder for a second if I really am awake, but this time I know I am. All my things appear to be in order, though I see that perpendicular to the wall with the washbasin, a burrow has been formed: a mound of blankets and coats, with a few thin cushions pushed together on the ground, fashioned into the likeness of a bed.

I search my mind for the last thing I remember, but my memories appear to be hiding from me. Fragments slide into view: a cherry-encased clock, porcelain piglets, unseen creatures in the bushes. Something seems to be about to come into focus, but I am too thirsty, too preoccupied with finding ways to alleviate the discomfort. My fingers grasp the air around me and I find a glass of water; the water tastes stale, or maybe that's my mouth, and my throat stings as the liquid goes down. My eyes feel stuck together so I rub them, a tacky white substance wiping off onto my fingertips, some of it coagulated into crumbs. While I am inspecting the residue, I hear movement from outside and my head jerks toward the door.

A figure appears, and with a jolt everything comes back to me.

"You're awake," exclaims Héloïse. She hurries toward me and sits on the side of the bed, placing her hand on my forehead; it feels steady and reassuring, like the hand of a statue. "I thought for a while you were never coming back." Her eyes are darting across my face, as though trying to make sure it is really me.

"How long was I—?" I hunt for the right word, but it's just out of reach.

"Five days," she says. I start to formulate another sentence but no words come; my eyelids feel like lead. She leans forward and strokes my hair, and I give in and fall back down into the bed. "Rest now."

*

When I open my eyes again, the consternation returns; for a minute I take in the room until little by little it all comes back to me. In the corner, the clattering of metal, the sweet smell of onions mingling with the odors that are emanating from me and my bed. I feel like I might need to heave again, but nothing is left. I maneuver my body upright, then drop one leg to the floor.

Héloïse hears my shuffling and dashes over, making sure I do not fall.

"Stay here," she says, steadying me on the side of the bed. "I'll bring you something to eat. You need to regain your strength."

I nod and do as she says. I feel depleted, like I am stranded on a precipice.

Héloïse approaches with a tray which she helps me balance on my lap, a warm bowl of vegetable soup in its center. After a second's pause she reaches for the spoon and I realize with mortification she is about to bring it to my mouth, so I shake my head.

"I can do it," I say, a little indignantly. Flashes of the preceding days threaten to rise up, but I do not want to remember. Not yet.

I move my arm toward the tray but it feels heavier than usual, not responding to my commands with the same readiness. But I will not back down; I grip the spoon and put all my concentration into each movement. I spill a few drops, but once I have swallowed the first mouthful I feel both ravenous and strong, the nourishment teasing me with a small taste of vitality. From there on, my hand moves more firmly, each spoonful easier than the last.

2

That evening, as darkness falls, we sit around the kerosene lamp. Now that my mind is less shrouded in fog and I have gathered some strength, Héloïse tells me about the days she spent at my side while I had the fever; how on the second day she was so concerned she asked the doctor to visit, a detail which surprises me. "You were—not yourself at the time," she explains tactfully. She shows me the medicines she has been breaking up into my food after I refused to take them.

"I'm so sorry I put you through that," I say. "Thank you—for everything."

"I'm just relieved you're feeling better."

"I didn't know you were coming. So you received my letter?"

"That's how I found you. When at first I didn't hear from you I thought something had happened." Her eyebrows knit together. "Why did you wait so long to write?"

I look down. In truth, I can't quite explain why I did not contact Héloïse or Antoine when the twelve months had elapsed. My days were spent high up in the mountains, near the sky, continuing my escape; I had tried not to dwell on my past life. It took me a long time to articulate to myself what I had gone through, to reflect on what those experiences had meant to me. It was only when that second winter came around, and my thoughts turned inward, that I had felt ready to send Héloïse a short note assuring her of my wellbeing.

I shake my head. "I'm sorry—I just needed time."

She nods, not entirely satisfied.

"How did you get here?" I ask.

"I spent the winter skiing near Lake Como with Eugène and the boys. I sent them back to Paris when I received a telegram about your letter, and made the journey here. It's a good thing I did, considering the condition I found you in."

I know she is referring to my fever, but I bristle. The lamp shines a warm and irregular light over Héloïse's refined features; branches creak outside, a low wind unsettling the forest. I consider reiterating that I had been doing well here before the illness, but I bite my tongue.

"What happened after you got on the train?" she asks softly.

My mind is cast back to that carriage, rattling and shaking through the night, the cramped and inconvenient bed. "I tried to get some rest," I start, my voice cracking slightly, as if out of practice. "But after everyone had gone to sleep I felt more awake than I have ever felt. The train was slow—it stopped at every small town." Everything had looked so still and beautiful in the dark; I couldn't believe it was really happening. "I waited until after the border, putting as much space behind me as I could. When it started to get light I knew I had to go. I got my things and waited until the next station—an industrial town, I forget the name."

I feel myself frown with concentration; it seems like such a long time ago. "I traveled inland, and went higher and higher until I reached a village. I rented a drab little room from an old woman at the edge of town." I close my eyes and can picture it completely: the crumbling stucco, the spatterings of mold, wallpaper peeling in the corners. Everything smelled stale and damp, like the air hadn't been changed in thirty years, but it was mine.

"I started to go for walks in the woods nearby, just easy hikes at first, but they quickly got longer. I stayed with the woman for a month or so, then traveled further up into the mountains." I think of the road winding along the cliffs, sitting in the carriage of a local visiting his family, until the air became clear and pure and I finally felt like I could breathe. "That's when I reached this village. I stayed in town for a few days while I roamed the mountains and the forest, until one day, on one of my walks, I found this cabin. When I arrived, I knew this was the place."

She gazes around the room, then back at me. "Are you happy here?"

A long pause. "Sometimes. Happier than I was, at least."

I think of her life waiting back at home; an inverted mirror of mine. I turn the question back to her. "Are you?"

She thinks for a little while, then nods. "Sometimes."

She holds my hand and we sit for a few seconds, watching each other.

"What happened after I left? How is Antoine?"

"Antoine is perfectly fine," she smiles. "He's doing very well in fact. He and Claude are good for each other, and we know that hasn't always been the case for him."

We exchange glances. "What does—he think happened?" We don't mention him by name. "Does he suspect you?"

"He did at first. He came to our house, full of accusations, but Eugène talked him down." Her eyes widen. "I had never seen him like that before—usually he seems so calm, so proper." Her grip on my hand tightens. My eyes are fixed on the table; it has been a long time since I've allowed myself to think about him.

"He was furious. He tried to get the police involved, sent letters to his cronies all over the country. Eventually got it into his head that you had run off with someone, and that this mystery man had organized the whole thing. He took a month or two off work to get to the bottom of it, and in that time one of his import deals fell through—another thing he blames you for, somehow." Her eyes dart up at me. "It was wise not to return to your home town, after all. I heard he sent his men there, asking questions."

I hesitate for a second. "And, what about…"

Héloïse glances at me, inspecting my expression as she speaks. "He did everything he could to be allowed to remarry in time, trying to find a legal loophole." A short pause. "He didn't manage," she says quietly. She purses her lips; the wind rattles a loose tile on the roof. "Your plan worked."

I had expected to feel victorious, but the news leaves me cold. I sense something dark and vast roiling beneath me, a wave waiting to engulf everything in its path; I can feel it lapping gently at my feet. We watch the flame in the lamp, flickering one second, blazing bright the next.

3

Once I have started to breathe more easily, we go for a walk in the woods. Winter, at last, is drawing to a close, and the first signs of spring are starting to become apparent. Héloïse walks through the forest with agility; trees look more vibrant around her, as though she is imbuing them with her own life force. In certain lights, the curious thought occurs to me that she has the lineaments and graceful movements of a deer.

"It really is beautiful," she says as we approach the pine tree at the top of the pass. Today its branches are a burnished nut-brown, the pine needles dark jade, birds singing from deep within. We sit underneath its shade and watch the peaks around us, the sky lilac and turquoise. "I can see why you've come here."

That night, when we are readying ourselves for bed, I hear a sound I have not heard in many weeks. I signal to Héloïse to remain silent, and as I go up to the door she huddles out of sight in the corner of the burrow.

The knock comes again and I open the door just enough for me to go outside, pulling it almost shut behind me.

"Evening." Vincenzo leans in to kiss me, and when he straightens up he reveals a bottle he has been hiding behind his back. He looks handsome, his pull magnified by absence.

"I can't, not tonight," I say. "I'm sorry." I mean it.

His smile falters. I see his eyes turn toward the shutters. "Is there someone here?"

"No," I answer, mindful of keeping my tone relaxed. Not being a natural liar, I revert toward the truth. "I haven't been feeling well."

He is not convinced, I can see it, but he assumes an expression of concern. "You do look pale," he grants, starting to appear genuinely alarmed. "Are you sure you're all right?"

*

I slowly grow stronger; I cook for Héloïse, demonstrating what I have learned of the ingredients that come from the local soil. I wish to show her my new world in its entirety, for her to understand my life here. I exchange places with her in our room, moving into the burrow so that she can have the bed. Every day, I try to find small ways to atone for the time she spent nurturing me back to life.

We have agreed to avoid being seen together in the village— an abundance of caution perhaps, but we are content, for now, with our solitary arrangement. In the mornings we have a quick breakfast, and every few days I go into town to pick up provisions while Héloïse goes down to the well. We meet back at the cabin and read or walk until lunchtime, when we prepare something together and, if the weather allows, eat outside on the fallen log.

Héloïse seems to have taken to this simple lifestyle, gazing at the forest in bemused wonder, but I know that the novelty will soon start to wear off. Back in Paris, it felt like she, Antoine and I had been alone together in the crowds, drawn magnetically to each other by a shared sense of distance from our surroundings. There was an incompleteness about us—a frustrated search for something—that had made us both deride and envy those for whom belonging appeared so effortless. But as the years passed, entropy had slowly drawn her toward the center of things, while Antoine was pulled toward a different, dazzling orbit. All the while, I had felt myself spiraling further and further out, connected by a string that was coming undone, one thread at a time, until I was entirely set adrift from the life I outwardly inhabited.

Every day that passes and my health is restored, I am increasingly aware that this cohabitation must come to an end, that Héloïse must return to the home she has created for herself. The evenings become filled with light, and we go for a final hike, to the highest point we can reach. The sun shines on every leaf, stone and stream; the forest seems to glisten, stirring again after a long sleep.

Back at the cabin, I prepare dinner with care, slicing artichokes, potatoes and garlic, sautéing them until they become fragrant. We eat in near silence, and when we have finished we sit opposite each other across the empty table.

"I have to return home tomorrow," says Héloïse.

"I know."

She looks up at me, her gaze steady. "When are you coming back?"

I hesitate. "Soon."

"You *will* be coming back, won't you?"

"Of course. I just need a little longer."

A pause. "I understand," she nods, and we embrace.

She packs her belongings and we prepare ourselves for sleep. Héloïse makes space for me in the bed; we lie curled up together, our bodies close and warm, my fingers lightly stroking her hair. I know I ought to feel guilty about lying to my friend about my plans. But as I lie there beside her, head buried in the pillow, my lips curl up into a gleeful smile. There are things I need to do here—things I must do on my own. I do not yet know their shape, nor what they will ask of me. But in the night I hear the forest calling, and I silently tell it I am on my way.

IV

1

I do not remember planting seeds last spring—not something one would easily forget, I shouldn't think. And yet, every day more flowers seem to appear in the clearing around the house, more intrepid weeds, more tender little shoots germinating green and fresh and undaunted by the astonishment with which I greet them. Purple crocuses yield their golden centers like a delicacy, blanched primroses sit demurely next to sky-blue for-get-me-nots, snowdrops hang like diminutive lampposts. Had they been here last year? I do not recall; perhaps I had been too preoccupied with my own thoughts to take much notice.

Whatever their provenance, I am glad of them: were it not for their company I would be quite alone these days, and while this is generally a satisfactory state of affairs I welcome the day-to-day variation they bring. From the damp muddy field left behind by winter, the earth surrounding the house has emerged anew; blades of grass appear more concrete—sharp, as though you might graze yourself if you fell on them. Soft tendrils twirl around the gnarls of the fallen log and instill in it the impression of life, tiny limbs emerging from the scabrous trunk. The decrepit tree leaning against the front window is decrepit still, but its desiccation has taken on a kind of mournful beauty: its branches are frail phalanges, reaching out with a yearning that puts me in mind of a consumptive heroine. From the inside, they intersect the sky in a way I find most pleasing, casting a pretty entanglement of shadows over the opposite wall, although it can't be denied that at certain times they can resemble thin iron bars. My assessment on the matter very much depends on what mood I have woken up in, but if I begin to be overwhelmed I have learned to remind myself of the duality contained in the scene, so that neither one feeling nor the other disturbs my day to any considerable extent.

My muscles feel weak after the period of enforced idleness. I pick myself up every morning as though moving through an invisible morass, waiting for my body to adjust to its newly vertical situation, for my mind to enter a murky and tentative consciousness. It is an hour or so before I am myself again, or something like it, and I venture out into the woods, the vigor scraped out of me and replaced by a slow but stolid determination. Day after day, my inability to get as far and as high as I used to frustrates me. At first I try to ignore the limitations, as if I could overcome them by stubbornness alone, but I soon learn to listen to my body. I find that if I am slow, I can go farther; if I pace myself, I can go higher.

Little by little, the snow is starting to melt away, its thick white blanket dissolving into isolated patches sparkling in the sun. The moist soil beneath smells clean and earthy, and I am more than once tempted to rub it between my fingers, feeling its grainy softness seep into me. I sit under the trees and listen to the sounds of the forest: birdsong, the low roar of running water. Wood cracks and creaks in the wind, the trees speaking to one another, answering, and calling out again. In the undergrowth there is furtive shuffling, the occasional muted squeak; chirps and cheeps and trills float through the air, a hypnotic symphony to which I am still learning the score. Sometimes, when I am listening to the trees, fatigue overtakes me and I lean back against a rock, sliding into unconsciousness.

Lately, when walking through the woods, I have found myself thinking more and more about the previous occupant of the cabin. I feel an affinity with him, somehow—perhaps due to our shared living arrangements, perhaps something else. There are times when, as darkness falls and the shadows thicken so that they seem almost corporeal, I think I see the soldier among the trees, but when I look again realize it is only a trick of the light.

*

The emptier my days become, the busier they get. No matter how much I seem to clean and scrape and tidy, it appears that there is always more cleaning and scraping and tidying to do, an inexhaustible supply of assignments I have no particular wish to attend to, but which I am always glad in the end to have completed. The broom feels stiff and splintery in my hand, bristles rasping hard against the ceramic, its retention of dust measly and erratic but ultimately sufficient if given enough application. Corners are tricky, so more often than not I end up getting down on my hands and knees and wipe the floor with a grimy cloth which I then shake outside, liberating the noxious particles into my still-sensitive lungs until I have coughed them all out into the ether.

I have become quite set in my ways, so everything has to be just so—the time I wake and the manner in which I prepare my food and tend to my house and body have to be very particular. If I sleep too late, or wear the wrong thing for the weather, the whole day becomes skewed, and no matter what I do I know that things will not go as I had planned and my thoughts begin to spiral, so I turn back to the point of the day in which the error was made, and I play it over and over again in my mind, castigating myself for my misdemeanor, then recreate the day once more but with that subtle change, showing myself how it might have been so much nicer, so much more perfect, if only I had eaten the fava beans rather than the fennel with my lunch, or waited to read Baudelaire until after five in the afternoon, or cleaned my plate directly after using it rather than leaving it to form a tenacious and unsightly stain, and then I think and think what a consummate idiot I have been, and how to improve my conduct the next time the occasion presents itself.

When things do not go to plan and my thoughts are in a whirl, a great lethargy falls upon me. There are times when I become stuck; a prodigious weight pushes down on me, immobilizing my limbs, a horrifying sense of dread overcoming me all at once, although I know it has been building little by little underneath the surface, and I sit and I stare and know I must move, but I am petrified, made of stone, and my thoughts swirl wildly inside me, drawing toward something terrible and nameless, and I know that if only I moved I could escape it but I cannot find the will to emerge from the depths, and I luxuriate in this feeling until it is sated, and having feasted on my energy it moves on, for now.

So, everything has to be done just as I like it; I know how I wish my days to unfold and I do not much like surprises to interfere with my plans. But despite my best efforts it seems as though there are fewer and fewer hours in the day in which to do things—I cannot imagine how I used to get everything done before, when I had appointments and schedules and events to prepare for, people to see, assignments to complete. I find that as soon as I have completed the bare minimum for the day, although I have woken at dawn and worked tirelessly hour after hour, suddenly it is dark again, and all the preparations for rest must be undertaken, with all the problems and unforeseen fluctuations in mood that those might entail.

And yet, as I toil and toil at the things that I am doing, and I am not altogether certain what those are a lot of the time, as the hours can run away from me, I do feel as though I am approaching—something—I am getting closer and closer to—

Well, we shall have to see.

2

Gianfranco's shop smells intoxicating, the aromas of meat and brine in perfect balance. It is close to midday, and while I await my turn I study each product with avid desire: half-moons of provolone, taleggio corrugated with mold, treacly caramelized figs, knobbly little buns which I imagine picking up and pulling apart with my hands, revealing a white and pillow-like interior. On the back wall, an oleaginous display of prosciutto legs, bisected for our scrutiny, each exhibiting its particular pattern of deep pink marbled with alabaster.

"Morning," I announce when my turn comes, exultant.

Gianfranco faces me, a certain vigilance in his expression. "How can I help?" No libidinous twinkle in his eye today, no leer grinning out from under his moustache. I am momentarily affronted, but then over the past weeks he has begun to regard me with a newfound seriousness. I consider making a joke, but I cannot think of anything that is neither stupid nor banal, so I say nothing.

We go through my order, and I feel myself straining to compliment his wares in a way that is both sincere and, frankly, rather close to pleading. "The pecorino I bought last time was truly exceptional," I am now saying, a note of desperation creeping into my voice.

Naturally, his response is to retreat. "Will that be all?" he says with formality, the expression frozen on his face; for a second, I think I detect the faintest trace of fear.

I nod, gather what's left of my dignity and settle up, cradling the savory parcels to my breast with tenderness. That final look lingers in my mind; when I first arrived here, I had put the villagers' distrust down to a perceived class difference between us—a surprising shift after my years of being looked down on in Paris, and one which I secretly welcomed. But their conception of me has altered somewhat; I sit too uneasily within that category, with my austere lifestyle and dwindling funds, and so they do not quite know what to make of me. Sometime over the past year, their wariness has slowly transformed into something darker, less easy to read.

As I step out into the street, I stop for a second in my tracks, as I always do when I see Vincenzo unexpectedly. We have not spoken since I turned him away that night, and I allow my eyes to rest on him from a distance before he notices me—a glimpse into another side of him, unguarded, more himself perhaps. He is deep in conversation with the gangly waiter from the café, who interjects a word here and there while Vincenzo continues with his monologue, a little annoyed, I can tell. I am not entirely certain I like this version of him; there is something cold about his demeanor I had not noticed before, or at least not fully acknowledged.

I consider turning and taking a longer route home, but there are too many people around and behavior of this kind would not go unnoticed. I keep my gaze on the street and march onward; I remind myself to straighten my back and lift my head, the whisper of my mother's voice echoing through my mind. As we pass each other, I glance at him and our eyes meet for a fraction of a second. The glance is too quick and too sudden for me to grasp anything of the emotion underpinning it, and yet as I walk onward I scrutinize it again and again in my mind, hoping to untangle some kind of conundrum, my thoughts in an unseemly spin.

My steps speed up on the pavement as I cross the road into the piazza, midday tolling from the bell tower. I inspect the people milling about in all directions, a tumult of activity before they disappear into their homes. Nuns in flowing habits flock toward the church, while gaunt-faced women shepherd children behind them; workmen sit on the edge of the fountain to smoke, eyes heavy with exhaustion. I hold the paper bag up to my face, inhaling the smells within like a hunter inspecting its prey.

I spot Mrs Barbieri across the square and lift up my hand to wave at her when a young man barges into me and I lose my footing. The bag flies out of my hands at a speed that is both exaggeratedly slow—my thoughts flash with all the things I could do to prevent the object's fall, with images of the steps that led me to this moment, each one conspiring toward the collision, or was it a push, and how things could have been different if only I had turned there, or stopped here, and I try to lunge forward to catch it while it still hovers in the air in front of me—and swift, inevitable: I know it is done.

The bag crashes to the ground, glass disintegrating, passata spattering my clothes.

"I'm so sorry, signora," whimpers the boy, hair falling limply about his face. "I didn't see you there." He crouches down to try and rescue what's left, but there is nothing he can do.

"Don't worry about it." I grit my teeth and attempt to compose myself; from his manner and the contrition on his face I am inclined to think the impact was inadvertent, although another part of me is not so sure. "These things happen."

I stand still for a few seconds and look down at the crimson stain on my dress, at the shards of broken glass, a whirlwind of emotions swelling up inside me. An elderly man walks up to me and asks if I am all right, and I nod, and he asks if he can help, and I smile politely and tell him I'm fine and inside I'm thinking why is it that men always offer to help precisely when they know they will be of no use, and I feel irrationally angry with the man, who is, to be honest, being perfectly kind to me, and I feel for a moment like I might scream.

*

That night, images from the day pass before my eyes as I lie in bed, some details sharpened, some distorted, others wholly elided, until I am not sure what happened, how I reacted, or how I ought to feel. Shapes move across the ceiling, shadows swaying in the moonlight, and I count backward from one thousand and attempt to clear my thoughts, waiting for that moment when I will drift into sleep, but as soon as I notice I am drifting—suddenly the spell is gone and I am once more awake, and I watch the shadows and count and drift and notice the drift and wake again, and then the shadows move and change and before I know it it is light, and I watch the ceiling and count until now it is fully, indisputably morning and the birds are singing so piercingly in the trees and I feel dazed and feral and my eyes are burning and finally, mercifully, I feel my lids close and a palliative drowsiness envelops my body.

When I wake again hours later, I do not feel refreshed; if anything, I am more worn out than before I climbed into bed. I pace back and forth as I try to lift myself out of my stupor, but my thoughts are sluggish and recalcitrant. I try to focus my eyes onto the pages of a book but the words enter my mind and sit there, sloshing about in an ebullient cauldron, waiting for me to pick them up before they dissipate into the pot.

It is raining outside, a noise I normally find calming, but today it feels like it is closing in on me. I put on my coat and step out into the clearing; I feel the rain fall on my face and all of a sudden I am eight years old again, when my mother would tell me off for walking around with wet hair, you'll catch your death, she always said, and I used to laugh until one day I fell asleep with my hair still damp from the sea, and I woke with a searing pain in my neck and face and back; she was triumphant, see, she said, *il colpo della strega*, the stroke of the witch. My skin starts to shiver and I turn back toward my cabin; my recent infirmity has shown me I am not impervious to the elements, not impervious at all in fact.

These last few months have unsettled me somewhat, I must admit. At some point during Héloïse's stay something seems to have altered—as though the air I move through is vibrating at a higher frequency, threatening to ignite at any instant. Perhaps it is a malignant after-effect of the fever; perhaps, whatever I was running from has finally caught up with me—it is difficult for me to say with any precision. But the past appears to have seeped through a membrane, infecting everything it touches, as though awakened after a long hibernation. The fragile stability I had reached has been upended, my thoughts thrown into disarray. Strange aches appear, then vanish. Small noises sound like the crack of a firearm. I forget simple things, then recall them with a start weeks later.

Back indoors, I pour myself a glass of wine but it tastes bitter, like it has soured after being left open too long. I stand up and check the door is locked; as I secure the key I become aware of the rickety windows, and for a second consider that it might after all have been better if those branches outside truly were iron bars. I feel drained after the previous night's contortions, so I climb into bed and close my eyes. But as soon as I am under the covers my heartbeat thumps fast in my chest, blood roaring in my ears, and I am more awake than I have been all day. I know this feeling well—as if I have forgotten how to sleep—it has happened before, and will continue to happen every night until I break the pattern, which could take weeks, perhaps more.

So I stare at the ceiling and prepare myself for another night of struggle—there is always a solution, I remember from previous bouts of sleeplessness. The problem is finding out what it is. I swaddle myself in voluminous layers and ready myself for rest: tea, blankets, a thick and impenetrable tome with which to dull my mind into an absence of thought, of being. Hours later, I am more alert than ever, every trick in my arsenal futile, each new position less comfortable than the last, until I have worked myself into a frenzy that knows it must sleep, but this knowledge only makes it all the more challenging to step over. And so it is morning again, but this time I do not fall asleep as I did yesterday, and my chest feels sore and every part of me aches, and I brush my hair and straighten my spine and rehearse my smile until it no longer gives away the maelstrom raging inside me.

*

Several more evenings pass in this manner, sapping my strength and perturbing my mind, before I admit defeat and turn to the solution I have been trying to avoid. While tiredness pours through me, a wail that demands release, a surge of adrenaline has come to attention, preparing for confrontation yet again. But what it hasn't accounted for is my liquid ally, the little bottle of laudanum I took with me when I fled. Something had drawn me to it—I knew it would have a role to play, even though I wasn't entirely sure what it would be: slow and steady physic or one-off solution. Over the past months I have rationed it with care, but I am at last nearing the bottle's end; one precious dose is left.

I twist its cap as if handling an inestimable jewel: it is resistant at first, the rim of the glass stiff with residue, but soon it gives way. I tilt it to reach the liquid at the bottom, dripping fifteen droplets of murky tincture into a glass of water. I swirl it around and wash back the bitter mix, coating the back of my throat with a flavor I detested at first, but which over the later years of my marriage I learned to associate with imminent relief. I sit back, my head rolling against the wall before falling to one side, a position in which I recline a while longer. A sensation of warmth and peace overcomes me; inner quietude, at last. I ease myself slowly under the covers, careful not to break the illusion; any wrong move, I know, risks undoing everything. As though shielding my eyes from the sun, I avoid thinking too directly about the necessity for sleep.

I look up at the ceiling and my eyelids become heavy, anchors sinking to the depths of the ocean, and there is nothing I can do now but wait, and breathe, and free my thoughts from the restraints of active control, letting the laudanum do the rest. I feel like I am floating—there are waves undulating beneath me, first to one side, then the other, and I concentrate on that movement, so soft and comforting, as though designed especially for this moment, and I am inside a cocoon and my body and thoughts are free of pain, and I am bathing in a sea of pearlescent, golden light.

3

The boy winds down the passageway, his steps as light and easy as an athlete's. He disappears around a corner and I hurry to keep up, glad when his silhouette is back in my sights. We emerge into an empty patio, the sounds of cooking clattering overhead. Sheltering under a doorway, he waits for me to join him; he is young, sixteen perhaps, his features angelic but his gaze unwavering.

He mumbles some numbers, lips barely moving, and I retrieve three coins from my purse. He gives them a cursory inspection and hands me a small parcel, which I clutch in my fist, the wrapper burrowing into my skin with a heavy and surprising intensity.

No sooner has the exchange taken place than the boy has gone, hastening down a narrow path in the opposite direction from the one we came. I look at the buildings around me to try to orient myself, but the sky is only just visible above the houses and I feel lost, trapped amid the brick walls and the clattering pans above. I take a few deep breaths and turn a corner, soon finding an alleyway filled with unfamiliar faces; I avert my eyes and trudge onward, back toward the streets frequented by those with nothing to hide.

After the previous night's sleep I feel luxuriant, my vitality restored enough that I might venture into the village without fear of a rogue movement or mannerism raising questions about my state of mind. I am afraid that my appearances in town in the immediate aftermath of my fever may have raised some eyebrows, and I have taken particular care today in my dress and grooming to reinstate the attitude of deference and mild intimidation that my initial arrival had been greeted with. I know better than to inspect the gazes of those I pass to appraise their reactions—such behavior would undermine all the brushing and combing from earlier this morning, the deployment of my fineries and my school-learned posture.

Of course, there is every possibility that, although I provided additional remuneration for his silence, the boy will spread news of my purchase far and wide—I envisage already the horrified miens of the churchgoing matriarchs, something that should probably fill me with apprehension but in truth I find rather appealing; let them be shocked, I think, they will never dare confront me about it. Their whispers I can deal with, as long as I can continue to come into town and bribe those I need to bribe, and purchase the few things I still need before disappearing again into the forest.

The late afternoon sun falls onto the cobbled streets, delineating each stone like pebbles on a river bed. The activity in the air is winding down; those who started their work with the rise of the sun are now at rest, the day's drudgery giving way to evening's worthy repose. My day, however, is only just beginning: in the mornings my body is in charge, muscles and sinews taking what they need from the day. It takes several hours for my thoughts to come into focus, and little by little they take one shape or another, showing me where my consciousness would like to take me for the night.

Back at the cabin I check for the parcel in my pocket, as I have been doing compulsively all afternoon. I open the paper wrapping to reveal a small, gleaming bottle, a replacement for the one I finished last night. Since my illness, much to my chagrin, I have found that alcohol has become acrid, its once exhilarating effects now enervating, but last night's laudanum offered a different form of escape. I pour it into a glass with some water, wash it down and feel a sweet soothing wave spread into my bloodstream. My limbs become soft and warm and heavy, my senses simultaneously dulled and sharpened. A few minutes later, feeling the need to be in open spaces, near vast skies and rustling trees, I get up and go outside to sit on the fallen log. The sun has gone down and the air is crisp and blue, and the view has never looked more beautiful.

*

I am lying in bed in a languid, pleasurable stupor when I am roused from my slumber by a rat-tat-tat at the door.

I open up and Vincenzo comes in, casting a furtive glance around the room, as if expecting me to have company.

We stand at a distance; I lean against the table, waiting for him to speak.

"I'm sorry," he starts. "The manager was there, I couldn't grab a bottle."

"That's all right. I'm not really drinking these days."

He looks at me, quizzical.

"I stopped when I got ill."

"Of course—are you feeling better?"

"I am now." I let the silence hang in the air.

"I'm sorry I haven't been around," he says. After a few moments it becomes clear no excuse is forthcoming, and I am relieved not to be subjected to some ill-conceived lie.

"It's fine," I say, suddenly tired, half-wishing I was alone again.

He comes closer. "I've been worried about you."

I look up at him as he puts a hand on my shoulder; it feels heavy and strong, sending reverberations through my body. I know already I will not be able to resist him, that I do not want to. He comes closer still and leans down to kiss me, and then his hands are on me and his body is pressed up against mine and I am no longer thinking about his excuses.

And then, he pulls back. He steps aside and picks up the small bottle from the table behind me. "You're still taking this?"

There is annoyance in his voice, which surprises me; after all, he didn't seem so opposed to the idea when he first used to come around.

"Maybe," I say, and let out a stupid giggle; I am more woozy than I had realized.

He is holding me at arm's length, his grip steady as if scolding a child.

"Are you going to tell me off?" I laugh, and he lets go of me, standing back.

"Where did you get this stuff?"

"In town." He had told me, a long time ago, where he used to get his. "I've been having trouble sleeping."

"You should be careful, you know—" he says.

"—people are going to talk," I finish his sentence, in a mock-lecturing tone.

We stare at each other for a second. A hard glint flashes in his eye, which arouses something inside of me.

"I'm serious," he says.

"I know." I walk toward him and stroke his arm gently; he does not push me away. "I do appreciate your concern. I really do." I kiss him, and he kisses me back.

Afterward, we are lying next to each other, his fingers drumming an absent-minded melody on my shoulders. We have not communicated anything overtly, but over the course of our love-making it has become clear it will be the last time; I hold him close, knowing we will have to speak soon, that it will complicate things. I inhale the smell of his sweat, its sourness stinging my nostrils and stirring my senses.

The drumming stops. "There was something I wanted to ask you," he says softly, in a way that appears calculated to sound casual.

"Yes?"

"The laudanum, you know—you didn't tell them I sent you, right?"

I sit up slightly. "What? No—I kept it vague. I paid the boy extra not to tell anyone."

Something in the way he looks at me suggests this has not been the case—that he already knew I had visited the boy; in a heartbeat, I understand this is why he has come tonight, of all nights.

"Just—it's better if no one knows about us," he adds, that casual tone again. "You know that."

I put my head back down on his chest, and the drumming resumes. "I know that."

We lie there for a while longer, in silence, and I realize two things at once. First, that this is partly what I had hoped for—I had thought that word of my purchase might reach him, that it might spur some kind of reaction from him so that I could see him again. I feel humiliated by this subterfuge, by my need for him, which he no doubt perceived and found gratifying.

The second realization feels like something is constricting my windpipe, an invisible pressure I try to swallow downward, to no avail. The reason he does not want anyone to know about our liaison has nothing to do with respectability, or scandal. As I lean against him, my fingers tenderly stroking the hairs on his chest, I understand that Vincenzo is ashamed of his visits to me in the night—that rather than being drawn to me and my particular qualities, he has been intoxicated by the power he holds over me, almost in spite of himself. Our relationship, with all that it meant to me, was a fabrication my mind had constructed out of fragments, a fiction he was happy to let me believe until it finally threatened to contaminate his own reality. Despite all his talk of feeling like an outsider in the village, deep down he is still part of it. I may have deliberately rejected that life, but along the way something about me has made it impossible to ever go back. Now, by the merest association with me, he himself would risk being tainted.

Through his eyes, over these months, I had allowed myself to believe in an idealized version of myself, the best parts of me amplified, my shortcomings softened. His validation had made me feel like someone deserving of—if not love, then an approximation of it. But in a few careless words, my careful construction has fallen in on itself, my worst fears about myself confirmed, my flaws distorted until they are grotesque and irredeemable. As I lie beside him, my body heavy and limbs numb, something peculiar starts to happen, a schism: it feels as though my consciousness is floating up toward the ceiling and watching the scene below with a sickening sense of vertigo. I am me, but not me—as if I were my own shadow, weightless and immaterial. I look down, separated from the vision of me I had seen refracted through Vincenzo, wrenched into something abject, that ought not to be seen.

4

The next day, as instructed, I get a dog. Well, not exactly—it is a little more complicated than that. Perhaps it would be more correct to say the dog found me. But I am not sure that is quite right either.

It's a cold morning, frost on the ground, birds screaming in the trees, that sort of thing. My fingers are stiff and jittery in my worn leather gloves as I climb the ramshackle wooden steps through the forest; my nose is raw from the wind and my eyes start to lacrimate—no matter how many times I wipe them with the end of my scarf it appears that more clammy liquid is ready to be secreted, so that soon I shall have no dry scarf left. I focus my attention on navigating the icy ground and do not allow myself to think.

I am still not quite awake. My muscles feel unusually heavy, my head aching after last night's laudanum—yet another vice I shall have to forgo, it seems. My attempts to fool my body and mind seem constantly to be catching up with me, but it is a struggle I am willing to undertake—I am not quite ready to face reality unfiltered. A little bit more self-deception would do nicely. If life reaches a point where it becomes unendurable, and you have exhausted every other means at your disposal, so you choose to trick yourself into temporarily obscuring reality, even just for a short while—and you are well aware that you are deceiving yourself, only putting off the inevitable dreadful return to the world as it really is—is that not simply survival? You know that the longer you stay away the harder the fall will be when you crash back down, and yet during those brief moments of escape, everything is blissful. But—perhaps it would be wiser not to dwell on such matters, or not to utter them at all. Let my moral ulcers and scars remain concealed behind that decent drapery of silence, as the English do.

So, as I was saying: ice, ground, birds. I rise up the mountain and direct my steps toward the plateau overlooking the ravine. There is something about that craggy outcrop clinging to the rock face, like barnacles on the edge of a monstrous sea cavern, that I feel drawn to today—a dramatic landscape to suit my mood. An indulgence that will not punish me for giving in to it the following day; a precious commodity, as we have seen.

The light has a uniform opaqueness, the sky obscured behind a milky film; wetness hangs in the air and on the tips of leaves like microscopic eyes. I pass pink clusters of rock jasmine, white uprisings of saxifrage, gentians' sapphire trumpets. I lean down and pick one of the trumpets from its orchestral swell, its obscene cavity gaping up at me. I take off a glove and hold the flower in my hand, studying the white and yellow dots within, like the markings of a tropical bird. I gently squeeze its fleshy stem, rubbing the sap between the tips of my fingers: it is sticky yet light, rich, life-giving, and I feel suddenly, horribly aware that I have severed it from the earth. I cradle its remains in my hand as though it were an injured parakeet, the beauty that had drawn me to it confronting me like an accusation.

I hold the flower to my chest and realize with some embarrassment that I am about to cry. I attempt to stymie my more melodramatic impulses, but it is no use—I am now sobbing, the full waterworks, and the knowledge of the outburst's flimsy catalyst aggravates it all the more. Finally, I am taking ragged breaths in and out, in and out, deeper and deeper until I have gathered my wits and clawed back a modicum of self-possession, and I am ready to continue my ascent. I feel lighter, the day less ponderous; the sun is starting to appear through the clouds. I laugh a few sheepish laughs to myself, which feel good in my throat, washing away the tension that had been lodged there in knots all morning. I straighten my back and wriggle my shoulders, and I am a whole new person.

By the time I have reached the plateau, the sun is higher, sending sharp shadows across the rocks and grass. Still, the mist enshrouds the precipice: I take a few cautious steps forward to look out at the ravine, but the ground feels precarious beneath my feet. I dare not advance any further. I sit on a rock in the middle of the field and open my clasped hand to inspect the flower. It has wilted in my grasp, the blue less resplendent, yet its petals retain their opulent markings. I lay the flower on the ground, but this feels too exposed to the elements—they are capricious today—and before I have had time to interrogate my motives, I have started to dig. I remove my gloves, then my hands are in the dirt and I am on my knees, frantic. I continue until the space seems sufficient and I place the flower in the pit, then stare at it for a moment before grabbing great big handfuls of earth to cover it up again.

Afterward I sit, breath fast and shallow. My hands are damp and grubby, fingernails black, the grainy residue lingering on my skin as though the soil is attempting to impart its vitality into me. I close my eyes and imagine it penetrating into my bloodstream; I place my hands back onto the ground, as though roots could form through them—thin capillaries connecting me to the mountain, my veins like inverted branches. If I could I would lie there and rest, and wait, and gradually be absorbed into the grass and the scree and the trees.

I stand up and wipe my hands on my dress, though they are still cold and stained when I thrust them back into my gloves. The mist has become looser, so I tiptoe toward the edge: I can now make out the ravine below, its stark rock formations, the deep crevice, steep angles like the earth has freshly split along a yawning abyss. Once I have seen what I came here to see, I turn back on myself, careful not to tread on the fresh patch of soil, and make my way toward the thicket bordering the plateau. The light is scintillating now, reflecting on the particles of water in the air so that everything appears luminous, the air radiant with dew.

I am within striking distance of the trees when I see it: muscle and speed, fangs, thick fur, yellow eyes staring into mine with menace. For the merest instant the thought crosses my mind that it is a large dog, but when I look again I know it belongs to the wild. I stop in my tracks and try to remember what I had read about surviving these encounters, but my mind is blank—ought I to make noise, or run, or stay extremely still—no way of knowing now. In any case, I am glued to the spot, eyes wide, limbs deprived of all volition. Behind me, there is open land and a precipice. Ahead of me, the narrow path that leads through the undergrowth is blocked by a majestic, glowering gray wolf.

We stand and watch each other; I wonder briefly where the rest of the pack may be. Then it comes back to me: I should make myself larger, maintain eye contact, attempt to back away—easier said than done, and at this moment, truth be told, I would prefer not to do any of those things. I think of the sheer drop behind me and take a deep breath, but then something changes, whether in me or the wolf I am not sure—whatever the reason, I feel compelled to stand still, precisely the opposite of what I had read. Gazing into the eyes of the creature in front of me, I am filled with a pervasive sense of peace.

She makes no move toward me, exhibits no sign of aggression. The more we contemplate each other, the less scared I become. What I had seen as menace now appears to me as pride; the fangs that had made my blood run cold no longer feel like imminent danger, but like armament. Then she turns toward the forest, stops for a moment to look back, and disappears with a few graceful leaps. I stand still for a few minutes longer, listening, waiting, but nothing seems to be lurking behind the pines.

That evening, and the next, I leave scraps of meat out in the woods beyond the clearing, an offering of sorts. In the mornings the scraps are gone, bones and all. Late at night I hear howling not too far from the cabin, throaty and mournful; a new development, I believe—but it is difficult, in these woods, to be certain of anything.

5

Employment has been more difficult to come by of late, but I find that I require less and less. My hunger has abated with the rising temperatures, and although my clothes are increasingly threadbare they are sturdy and durable, and where they come apart at the seams I stitch them back up—I do not mind the patches of mending; I think they rather add character.

The flowers outside my house are growing lusher and more bountiful by the day. I have been reading up on sprouts and seedlings, and in my ever-rarer trips into the village—largely, these past few days, to procure meat for my offerings—I ask the locals for their expertise on the matter, one thing they are happy to dispense free of charge. In the mornings I get to work, sowing and planting and raking and watering and all the rest of it, and in a matter of days I have planted spring flowers and root vegetables, berries and herbs.

I start to leave water and slices of food at the edge of the clearing, and watch as doves and blue tits descend on them, pecking delicately at the ground; if I am very still and very quiet, rabbits and hares emerge from the darkness to nibble on what is left. At dusk and dawn, I have once or twice seen roe deer's white rumps materialize from the cover of the trees. Some chickens have made my yard their home; I feed them grain and pieces of fruit, which they repay with a generous supply of eggs in a nest under a nearby shrub.

After dinner, when the weather is fine, I turn down the lights and sit outside the cabin, listening to the crickets' repetitive mechanical calls, the spectral hooting of owls, the trees' gentle creaks and sighs. My reading has gradually fallen away—I suspect, more and more, that the answers I seek do not lie in the books and journals I used to parse for meaning. I find myself gravitating toward an absence of words, written or otherwise; perhaps, in this way, my thoughts might be disarmed of their sting. After some time sitting in silent meditation, my breathing regularizes into a slow and steady rhythm and my body becomes both heavy and weightless, drawn equally to the sky and the earth, and the turmoil in my head is for a few moments replaced by a pure inner stillness, clear as a mountain stream. On nights when the noise is still too loud and I need the silence to be complete, I obliterate myself with laudanum and fall into a deep and unfeeling sleep.

*

One morning, when I am returning from the top of the pass, I slip on a patch of mud and the sole of my walking boot comes apart from toe to heel. I stagger down the mountain, pain shooting up my foot with every step I take, a pool of blood starting to bloom along my thin gray stocking. At the cabin, I do my best to sew the boot back together, but after several attempts concede defeat. I unlock the drawer where I keep the money and count my remaining bills: Héloïse left some behind when she left, despite vehement protestations on my part, but I can see now that it will not last much longer.

Down in the village, I purchase a second-hand pair of boots, not quite the cheapest but inexpensive enough to leave me with change. I am muttering some calculations to myself as I walk through the streets when I realize I am approaching the pharmacy. The bottles and jars glint in dull, orderly rows, a reminder of all the ways bodies can turn against those who inhabit them. I shudder as I always do when I walk past, as if sickness could pass into me through the glass, infecting my insides like a rot.

Although I had not planned to, I notice with alarm that I have stopped, and have opened the heavy metallic door with a clank.

Once inside, I take small, shallow breaths, attempting to avoid the fumes in the air. The apothecary is speaking to a customer, so I cast my eyes around the shop, inspecting the different vials and pomades. I recognize one or two beauty products I used to buy when money was no object, and to distract myself from some of the memories associated with those days—not especially pleasant ones—I start to hum quietly in the corner as I peruse the shelves.

I see that the apothecary is watching me, and so I smile at him graciously.

"Signora Mantovani," nods Mr Barbieri, before returning his attention to the man at the counter.

When my turn comes at last, I engage in a little polite conversation. "How are Alberto and Enrico?" I ask, somewhat distractedly; my eye has been drawn to an ominous bottle at the back with a particularly toxic-looking label.

"They're well, thank you." He does not go into detail. He glances at the line behind me, then gently asks, "What was it you were looking for?"

"Oh," I start. "I don't suppose you have any—" I pause, searching for a likely explanation for my presence in the store. I pick up the smallest item in front of me, a box of honey lozenges. I affect a feeble cough. "—throat sweets? I've been looking for them everywhere."

As I pick out a coin from my purse, I add, almost as if it were an afterthought, "And—you do not happen to have any translations you need doing, do you?"

"I'm afraid I don't, no." He lifts his shoulders in an apologetic shrug.

I laugh at this, too loud, and swiftly curtail the sound. "Well, that is no problem. It is only that I find them stimulating, you see—keeps my mind sharp. Makes a change from reading in the evenings, that is all." To change the subject, I say, "I saw a wolf on the plateau the other day."

His eyebrows corrugate into a frown. "You should report seeing one so close to the village. They're very dangerous."

I stand back. "I am really not sure that is necessary. Besides, the mountain is as much hers as it is ours."

"Very well, then." He shares a glance with the other customers. "Is there anything else I can help you with today?"

"That will be all. Thank you very much." I pick up my things and turn toward the door. As I look around me, I am strangely surprised that the people in the shop seem to see me; I feel as though I am not really there at all.

*

On my way back to the cabin, I take a detour to the well to fill the bucket I had left there before coming into the village. The glade is still and quiet, the rays of the sun turning the trees' branches a glowing orange hue, as if tinged with an inner light. I get the sharp, sudden sensation that they are on fire; but when I stop and look again, closer this time, they have transformed back into green pines in the evening sun.

I lower the bucket, the damp and cold of the well palpable against my skin. I look down, breath labored from working its rusty mechanism, and see that light pink curl again, larger now, joined by many more: fungus-like growths sprouting in patches among the bricks, rosy and delicate—almost like flowers, from a distance. I realize that I have stopped rotating the pulley, the bucket suspended in mid-air. I lean closer, and closer, until my balance almost gives way and I take a step back, legs trembling. I peer down again, hands firm on the edge, and see that the bottom of the well is overgrown with this lichen, thousands of rose-colored spirals, swirled and interwoven and reaching up from the shadows.

But even as I watch the intricate shapes, I cannot be altogether sure that they really are attached to those bricks. Even though I can see them clearly with my two eyes, I cannot discount the likelihood that the next time I come by they will not have mysteriously faded away again. This has started to happen with increasing frequency: streams appear to vanish overnight, trees change into entirely new shapes between one walk and the next. A disconcerting occurrence, though usually benign. I am more distracted than usual these days, it must be said.

In truth, I have started to rather doubt my own senses of late. More than once, I have seen figures among the trees that vanish as soon as I turn my eyes on them, heard intruders in the night that are later revealed to be leaves brushing against each other—but, for that fraction of a second, the two realities coexist. Of course, what I see does normally correspond with what is in front of me. But, over the course of these months, I have started to wonder whether that is always the case.

6

My second spring here reveals patterns and details I had not noticed before. I move by instinct, going where my senses desire: I smell the honeyed scent of flowers and kneel to savor their perfume; I hear a stream and turn toward it, immersing my hands in the crisp sibilant water; my eyes are drawn to ferns unfurling their mesmerizing fronds. I find new ways through the forest—higher, wilder, deeper. I feel like I could walk in these mountains a thousand years and still not fully understand their mercurial beauty.

One day, I hunger for the hard purity of granite cliffs, which cleave as close to the sky as it is possible to do. I have seen them from a distance—they are beyond the limits of where I normally venture, but I direct my steps toward them and find a new way through the trees. I do not know whether I shall be able to reach them, or what I hope to find there, but I weave through the firs and larches until I reach the treeline. I step out into the open: above me there is only sun and rock and sediment, the light assaulting my eyes from all sides, and as I advance my feet slip and I graze my knees and palms against the rough ground.

I go on, feet aching and legs sore, a dryness in my throat that will not be quenched by water. The pass is just starting to be visible up above, my need to reach the summit increasingly frenetic. Oxygen reaches my lungs with uncertainty; it grazes the surface rather than suffusing them throughout. The sun has long passed the highest point in the sky, but it does not matter. I am too close now—the adrenaline overpowers all the parts of my body that are screaming for it to stop.

After remaining at a steady distance from me all this time, the pass has come closer in one breathtaking instant. The final stretch goes like lightning, my limbs rippling with speed. I scramble across the top into an arid vista: no intrepid flowers sprout here, just the blinding glare of the sun against the serrated granite rocks.

Everything is perfectly still, except for the clouds moving with unthinkable velocity; everything is perfectly quiet, except for the wind crashing against the cliffs with its volatile and simmering power. Something moves above me and I shield my eyes: an enormous bird soars in the air, wings and body still while its tail steers against the wind, painting fluid circles in the sky. It flaps its wings once, twice, and continues its sinuous flight before it is joined by another; they soar together, then one descends and loops around the other, wings almost touching. I watch the eagles until they are dots in the distance, disappearing against the darkness of the forest below.

The shadows on the rocks are getting longer, and I know I must return. When I get to the edge and look down, I feel a wave of sick threatening to rise in the back of my throat; the angle looks a lot steeper from this direction. I try to determine which part of the forest I came from earlier, but it is difficult to tell from here. I fasten my bag to my back, and put first one foot on the scree, then the other, keeping my body sideways and digging in my heels. By the time I reach the treeline, the sun has already started to set. The day's efforts have taken their toll; I badly need rest. The place at which I have re-entered the forest is unfamiliar, and the light is too soft now to see under the thickening canopy. I reproach myself for losing track of time; complacency got the better of me, a dangerous trait in the wild.

I am too tired to go on much longer, and will not make it back to the cabin before nightfall. I make use of the waning light to find a sheltered spot, a rock overhang under the roots of a great oak tree; it seems dry and hidden, a few vines hanging over the front, partly masking the entrance. I pick up a stick and nudge the space to ensure it is unoccupied, then position myself in the hollow. My neck cranes toward my bag, a hard and uneven pillow, the ground beneath me coarse with dirt and rocks. In the air I hear the low calls of owls, hidden among the trees, as the soft darkness envelops everything in sight. I wrap my coat around me, close my eyes, and try not to think about vipers.

*

When I open my eyes, I am sure I am still in a dream. It is a clean awakening, one in which your eyes open instantly and your mind is alert, even though some information is still out of reach. For the longest time I do not remember where I am, or the events of the previous day, and I watch in amazement at the shimmering beauty of the view that meets my eye. Swaying vines, monumental oak trees, the dappled greens of leaves and pine needles: the forest is like new to me, as if I were seeing it for the first time. When the details of my identity finally come into focus again, the spell is not broken, but redoubled, as though I were seeing the forest through two sets of eyes.

Despite the efforts of the previous day's climb, I feel no soreness in my body, as if I had slept on a bed of silk and feathers; my movements are smooth, roaming intuitively through the trees. While I do not know the precise path, I see now where I ought to go. I come across a plant of wild strawberries, stalks heavy with fruit; I kneel to pick a handful and eat them leisurely, their flesh melting in my mouth.

The birdsong is unusually mellifluous: trills and whistles like molten amber, exuberant calls of pure joy. Colors appear more vivid in this part of the forest, the greens deeper, the browns richer, flecks of sunlight dancing on the undergrowth. Emerald dragonflies buzz past, delicate wings glittering. Everything appears alive, connected; if I stop to inspect a plant or flower, I seem to be able to detect a gentle motion of ebb and flow.

The weather is mild, so I remove my coat and slacken the buttons of my shirt; I untie my hair and let it fan around me—I have a need to feel the forest on my skin. Something compels me to adjust my steps slightly, and I follow that impulse toward a path that has appeared through the trees until I hear the sound of water, a vision of sunlight shimmering in the distance. As I get closer, a lake becomes visible between the pines and I am leaping across the forest floor, drawn as though by tidal force.

The lake is a color I have never seen before: verdigris, perhaps, and aquamarine, but with a transparent quality that transfigures it into something else entirely. A fluorescent luminosity dances across the water, which appears lit from within, the surface glimmering thickly like quicksilver. On the far shore it is surrounded by dense pine forest, bordered on the side by a grassy knoll. A scattering of pebbles shines through the crystalline surface around the lake's edges before giving way to that astonishing color, reflecting a fractured likeness of the surrounding mountains.

I unfasten my clothes. I can see no one around, and even if there were anyone I doubt it would have stopped me. Everything comes off, and my feet are in the water, then my thighs, and I bring my hands together in front of me and dive, submerged in liquid light. I swim deep into the blue-green jewel, clear and cold as the middle of an ocean. I come up for air, spin and release a wave of gentle splashes. I take in the sun, the vast sky, and hear something buzz near my head. I turn to see it but it is too quick; it sounds like an insect, but is much too large. And there it is again—I turn toward the noise and a tiny bird is hovering near me. It moves before I can examine it, its bright chirp unknown to me, and I turn again and this time I see it clearly. Until now I have seen one only in paintings or books from faraway lands, but there is no mistaking it—a single iridescent hummingbird, one second lilac and green, the next blue and pink. For a few seconds, I forget to breathe.

As soon as I have identified it, it flies away. I splash around a little longer, lost in thought, trying to remember whether—but never mind. I should get back to my things. I turn onto my back and float for a few seconds longer, the sun's warmth infusing my body, before swimming ashore. The pebbles gleam invitingly at the bottom of the lake: opals, malachite, lapis lazuli. I pick up the most dazzling and bring it to the surface, but as soon as it slips above the water it turns again into a pebble, smooth and gray.

I cast aside the stone and step onto the shore. I watch the lake as the sunlight dries my skin; everything appears quiet, pristine. I must tell someone in the village about that hummingbird, I think, as I watch a prehistoric-looking lizard sun itself on a nearby rock—ask whether they are normally seen in these parts. But, as soon as the thought crosses my mind, something else inside tells me I ought not to.

*

Back at the cabin, things have changed significantly overnight. The vegetables and herbs whose seeds I planted have started to germinate, rather faster than I had anticipated, so that the plants are nearly fully grown—and there are, if I'm not mistaken, a few I did not plant at all. Flowers and plants have flourished into ornate bushes, some climbing the cabin's walls, others spreading across the grass. Their leaves are lustrous, sparkling in the warm light; petals pulsate, vibrant and electric, almost as though they were breathing. Patches of wildflowers have sprouted where before there was only dirt.

I put out more food and water at the side of the clearing, and before long two hedgehogs have arrived, a marmot, a badger. The silhouette of an enormous eagle owl comes into view before disappearing again, its ears like pointed horns. As I watch, three cockatoos fly past and flitter about, crests curled upward like dainty primrose gloves.

Inside, the cabin remains largely unchanged, but through the window the tree is more human than ever—a woman, evidently, leaning back in a weary pose as if expecting to be caught before a fall. Taken by a sudden impulse, I inspect my reflection. In the mirror, I am a goddess: my face glows like a Greek deity, hair curled and regal, my outline surrounded by a halo of quivering golden thread. I watch the reflection for a few moments longer, trying to find myself under the veneer, but I can't untangle the two; they appear to be one and the same.

Outside, something is stirring at the edge of the woods; the trees rustle in the soft wind. All around, the margins of things start to blur and bleed into one another. At the tip of every leaf and blade of grass a series of diaphanous swirls appears to be spreading outward. I sit on the fallen log, now covered in green shoots, and watch the changing light: the sunset is effulgent, coating the distant peaks in molten gold. Scarlet clouds come together and dissolve before my eyes, refashioned into geometric configurations that replicate into infinity, kaleidoscopes of stars and moons and seraphim blowing trumpets in the sky.

V

1

I start to walk farther, longer. I am less constrained by my need to return home every night, as shelter is available whenever I am in need of it. I have attempted, without much luck, to retrace my steps toward the lake where I first saw the hummingbird, but despite my efforts I cannot seem to locate it. The woods seem to have taken on unusual colors—not just deeper but slightly off. Certain tree trunks appear a lurid purple; tangerine and teal leaves wave in the breeze. Miniscule crystals have started to grow on rocks and trees, covering surfaces in fine diamond-like granules, bioluminescent in the moonlight. Everything appears wilder, more intense; a sense of excitement and danger hovers at the edges of things.

Something has happened to me since that night in the forest, as though the world has gained an additional layer: it is a peculiar thing to experience, and almost impossible to describe. It has been happening for some time, to tell the truth, but there is no mistaking it now. In a way, it is as though I have become possessed of a double vision—mine and another's, at once, so that each look holds both prior knowledge and the wonder of newness, or—that is not quite right. But it will have to do.

I stop eating meat, then cheese. I have an abundance of food around the house, so I find that I hardly need to go into the village at all. Eggplants and olives grow bountifully among the vegetables; plump lemons and oranges, as sweet as any from Sicily, flourish in the trees that have appeared. Anything that my garden does not provide, the forest does: nuts and mushrooms and berries are plentiful wherever I direct my steps, so that I am rarely at a loss for food when I am on my walks. Although I no longer leave offerings out for the wolf, I hear her call at night and know she is near.

I am running out of money, but it does not matter. I am wholly preoccupied, now, with the curious changes that are happening around the clearing. After the trip to the lake, I continued for a while to go about my business as before—going into town for provisions, fetching water, chopping wood. But then, the food began to replenish itself. Fresh piles of logs would appear when I wasn't looking, buckets of water become full again overnight. The changes affect organic matter only, I have noticed; anything man-made appears to remain untouched.

One morning, I wake to a deafening squawk and find a peacock strutting outside. He inspects me with exaggerated hauteur before continuing his deliberate and imperious walk, long silver feet stepping elegantly over the grass. As the weather grows warmer, flies and insects buzz in the air with their multifaceted eyes, while spiders weave exquisitely complex webs. Butterflies flutter by with a flash of electric blue; when they alight on a branch, their wings stare back with the eyes of an owl and the body of a snake—elaborate markings, I read somewhere, designed to make them resemble their own predators.

In the clearing, flowers blossom that I do not recognize, and which are not listed in the local almanacs, more baroque and tropical than any I have seen: dahlias, passion flowers and orchids, alien-looking blooms shaped like dancing maidens and birds of paradise. No matter how long I leave them on the plant, fruit and vegetables are ripe at the moment of picking; grapes of varying color sprout from the vines even though autumn is still months away. I make flatbreads on the stove from my supplies of flour and olive oil, which do not seem to diminish despite daily use, and want for nothing else.

And so I am more free to walk, and sit, and listen to the forest. The more I listen, the more it speaks. I have not yet heard its voice, but surely it is only a matter of time.

*

A month has passed, I think, from my swim in the lake, though time percolates differently these days. If my calculations are correct, my rent is overdue. This puzzles me, as both so much and so little has happened since my last visit to the village: it seems impossible for hours to pass in an instant, but for weeks to linger on far past their allotted duration. Or perhaps it is the other way around.

I collect what is left of my savings, enough to pay for several months of lodging in advance, and tuck it into an envelope. I make no special effort in my dress; I am no longer interested in what the villagers think of me. Besides, I am convinced that the transformation that has taken place has changed something fundamental in me—for the better, that is—and that this will be plain to anyone I come across. My shoulders feel straighter, my head higher, my movements possessed of an easy grace.

On the way into the village, the wind picks up. My hair is loose around me, blowing in all directions, but I do not reach up to tame it; my face and vision are left clear, and I enjoy the way the gale feels on me. My body is strong and heavy as it cuts through the air like a knife. I cross the bridge after the Rossettis' farm and the first villagers come into view, hunched and cowering, defeated by a breeze, hats held tight and belongings flying.

My steps are slow and resolute as I walk down the cobbled streets. Scurrying like frightened ants, the people around me appear defenseless—it is almost touching. I can barely remember the time when I would creep through back alleys for fear of their censure. Once I have reached the middle of the piazza, I pause for a few moments, watching the chaos unfold around me. As I stand, a man runs past, shouting, "There's a storm coming, lady, you should go home." He gets closer and looks up at my face, then frowns slightly. "Oh—I'm sorry," he adds in a small voice, and hurries away.

So something has changed—good. Let them be afraid. I turn my head to one side, then the other, feeling the bones in my neck and shoulders crack into place. A few people are staring now, but they do not meet my eye. It does not matter—I neither know them nor do I have time for their meddlesome and superstitious ways. I have come down here for a reason, and so I turn in the direction of the palatial home of my landlord. I rap at the door and am let in by his maid, or is it his wife, she does not say, merely points upstairs.

He is sitting in his study, gray hair and a white beard like bristles on a broom, reading a thick leather-bound book. Sensing me approach, he sets it down. He appears cautious, though not noticeably alarmed.

I hand him the envelope. "Six months of rent."

He reaches out and, just before his fingers touch the paper, pauses, and looks at me as though he is on the verge of saying something. But before the words stumble out of his lips he stops himself.

"I hope the cabin continues to be satisfactory," he says, pocketing the envelope.

"It's everything I need," I reply, appreciating his courtesy and discretion. A swift, pleasing transaction, this—if only others would be so considerate. I disappear back down the stairs.

The wind outside has mounted to a frenzy; it can't be long until the rain comes—everything feels suspended. Once I am at the edge of town I breathe deeply, leaving behind civilization and being welcomed once again into the mountain's cold and mighty embrace. I have no further need for the village or its inhabitants: I seem to have passed over into—somewhere I am no longer beholden to the chains and responsibilities of man, but to the perfect harmony of the natural world, where everything has its place, and no rock or broken twig is without purpose.

The rain is starting to descend as I rise along the path and through the woods, and although the water falls upon my hair and clothes it slides off again onto the ground. Like the larch and the pine and the stone, I am not afraid of rain: its touch is life itself. I smell the soil and the streams; I see the moss and the grass turn up toward the heavens and rejoice.

*

Hours later, as I am listening to the rain on the leaves, I hear footsteps outside. I am up before he knocks, and open the door to find Vincenzo approaching, his coat held over his head.

We stand still for a few moments. The situation feels familiar, but the quality of the air between us has changed. "Can I come in?"

I move aside, careful to avoid brushing against him. "Be my guest."

He walks in and shakes his hair and torso, showering drops around him on the floor.

"How can I help?" I ask, inclining my head to one side. I had thought he might come by one of these days, so I am unfazed to see him at my doorstep after all these months.

"I'm sorry to drop in like this." He folds his coat, holding it awkwardly in front of him. "I wanted to talk to you. I saw you in the square earlier."

"Oh." I had not noticed him; even now, his physical proximity has no effect on me. "And you're sure no one saw you coming here?" I furrow my brow with a show of concern, remembering his casual inquiries last time—his fear of contamination.

"No one saw me." He shakes his head, looking serious, and moves his coat from one hand to the other. He takes a deep breath. "I feel bad about how things ended between us. I'm sorry. I know I didn't handle it well."

I exhale slowly. "Is that all you've come here to say?"

He pauses. "Well—there is something I want to tell you. Before you find out from someone else."

I nod, watching the droplets pool on the ceramic tiles beneath him. "What is it?"

"I'm—getting married," he says at last, with an apologetic little smile. "I want to do things right this time. I thought you should know."

"How gallant." I have nothing else to add.

He is scrutinizing my face, as if trying to solve a riddle.

"So what is this?" I snap, momentarily annoyed. "You're visiting all your former conquests to share the happy news?"

"No." He raises his eyebrows, moving slightly back. "It's not that. I just wanted to tell you personally. So I could see—well, how you would react. That you wouldn't..." His voice trails off.

I nod. "Go on."

He puts up his hands. "I don't know—that you wouldn't make some sort of scene."

I have never seen him so nervous; I am enjoying watching him squirm. "Why, how did you think I would react?" I lean back, gazing at him. "Would you rather I was devastated?"

"N-no," he stutters. "Of course not." He starts fidgeting with his hands. He waits for a few moments, as though expecting me to ask further questions, but I find to my surprise that I do not particularly care about the details.

"I'm glad you've taken it so well," he says finally, consternation and relief alternating across his face. He gestures toward the rain. "I'd better get going."

I walk him out, then step aside to let him pass; we watch each other on the doorway. "So you're becoming a local after all these years," I say with a small smile. "Congratulations, I suppose. I hope you find whatever it is you're looking for."

He stares at me intently for several seconds. "Thanks, Laura. I really hope you do, too."

2

For ten days the rain falls, interspersed now and then with the resounding crash of thunder, lightning's coruscating glare. The clearing around my cabin is spared the worst of it, but in the adjoining areas all is mud and water: rivers overflow their banks; water saturates the earth; silt and rocks conjoin into landslides which leave great gashes on the hillside. I understand these processes are natural, necessary perhaps, but it pains me to watch my surroundings so transformed. I spend these days inside: the mountain is too dangerous to roam, something tells me, for now at least.

When the rain stops, it feels like a different kind of rebirth. For a few days the ground feels unsteady, as though it has become detached from the rock beneath. Birds and animals appear reluctant to emerge, lest the rain begin again without warning. I inspect the flowers and plants, which are largely undamaged, but further afield the changes are more noticeable: paths have been obscured, branches snapped, flowers sodden and crushed. Several birches have fallen in the woodland, their elegant silver trunks languishing on the forest floor. The physiognomy of the landscape has been altered, but if my time in the cabin has shown me anything, it is that the mountain is in a continual state of flux. And so the sun shines and dries the earth, reviving the flowers, and the process continues. The days grow longer and I resume my walks, finding new routes and hidden corners; my garden yields ever more elaborate crops. The peacock, who had gone into hiding during the rain, returns to his prancing perambulations. The sunlight turns my skin from waxy pallor to a soft golden glow. The fallen birches in the forest, now covered in moss, become a home to lizards and shrews.

It seems as though this state of grace might continue forever. But days pass, and weeks, and then it has been a month since the last rainfall. Summer is reaching its zenith; the sun shines inexorably in the sky. Clouds form, a tantalizing display, but do not amass enough force to consolidate, and they dissolve once more. The earth grows drier and less compact, dusty now; previously supple flowers wilt and droop. Crops fail, their leaves shriveled and wan. Small fires start, then bigger ones. Life-giving forces turn deadly, fickle gods toying with those they watch over. I look to the clouds again, but no angels appear this time, nor rain.

*

One afternoon, I return to the cabin after a walk to find it defaced. A series of scrawls has appeared on the walls outside, crude messages meant to intimidate and offend: witch, bitch, hag—not very imaginative, I must say. I have called myself much worse. They appear to believe, from what I can decipher, that I exert a degree of control over the elements, which I must say I find rather complimentary. Less pleasingly, one of the windows has had a rock thrown through it. I unlock the door and sweep up, wedging an old rag into the fracture. I warm some water and scrub the writing with a soapy dishcloth, a reminder of my first days here. I try to recall whether the prior messages had been worse than these, but it is harder to bring to mind insults not aimed at oneself.

I prowl the woods around the clearing, searching for clues. Everything else, for now, appears to be in order. I griddle some vegetables and sit at the table, trying to gather my thoughts, once again peering warily through the windows at the bushes outside. The forest appears as it was, but different; I can't trust it, not as much anyway. I am not afraid, exactly, but I feel unnerved by the intrusion into my space. I had thought that by abstracting myself from society I would eventually be forgotten, maybe regarded as a curiosity, but people seem intent on reminding me that escape is an illusion. I feel the residue of my previous life on me like a stain.

But I am not who I was. I shall not let them prevail. I make sure the door is locked, close the shutters and ready myself for bed. I have more important things to worry about, you see. Very important things indeed. Only, it continues to be difficult to put them into words—as if the right words have not yet been invented. Perhaps it will turn out they are not words at all. So I am doing my best with what is available to me, black squiggles on a white page, mere echoes of the extraordinary things that are happening around me.

3

A few days later, clouds form in the sky; before long the rain comes, but this time it does not linger. A precarious equilibrium is restored. Summer continues its soothing advance, lengthening the days and softening the night air with sweetness, a heady humidity that overwhelms the body and ensnares the mind.

I have, over these months, grown exceedingly fond of each flower, plant and tree in my clearing, and I believe the sentiment is returned—inasmuch as it can be, of course. I greet my tomato plants in the mornings, and I tell them about my plans for the day. My mode of address toward tropical flowers is one of respect and flattery, a bit of learned discussion about the arts, while the potatoes prefer a more informal repartee, even the odd rude joke or two. They are my companions, after all, and I value their presence above all else. So letting them know how I feel seems the only reasonable, and polite, thing to do. Sometimes, if I am to tell the whole truth, I even sing to them: silly little songs derived from those of my childhood, the words amended for the occasion, other times ditties of my own invention.

My journeys away from the house become longer: I roam the mountains and lakes for two, three nights at a time, meandering wherever my feet see fit to take me. I have slept in caves, in meadows, under waterfalls. But if I stay away any longer than that, I am gripped by a deep longing for my garden and its inhabitants. The flowers in the woods are not particularly chatty, you see, and I miss the conversation.

The forest continues to astonish me with its richness. I love, more than almost anything else, to lie on its floor and gaze up at the canopy for hours at a time, watching each tree's particular arabesque of leaves and branches, helixes warping and spiraling overhead. Water continues to exert a powerful hold over me: the sight of a lake's shining surface can be enough to wash away days of accumulated tension, while bathing in its waters reconfigures my thoughts anew. Then there are times when nothing but the most strenuous exercise will do, when I push myself as hard and as far as I can go, then go farther. By the evening, my body is heavy and my thoughts are light.

Every now and then, regrettably, I run into other people on my walks, though I do my best to turn the other way or, if a suitable spot is within reach, hide. In fairness, they do not appear especially pleased to see me either. One little girl burst into tears when she saw me approach, as her parents apologized over and over. An elderly couple mumbled to each other as they passed, shaking their heads with displeasure at something or other. Some pretend not to see me at all. But for the most part, I grin a wide grin and doff my cap, if I am wearing one, and they smile and nod and hasten their footsteps.

*

Back at the cabin, I unload my bag and clean my clothes in preparation for the next trip. In between excursions I prefer to stay home a while, exchanging bon mots with the asparagus and luxuriating in my little paradise until I feel the need to head back out into the woods. But there is less distinction, these days, between home and wilderness.

My twofold vision comes and goes, becoming stronger or less pronounced at different hours of the day, like changes in the weather. I study leaves to see if they remain in their original state or if they lengthen and multiply, duplicating into ever-smaller patterns; I watch ordinary-looking petals metamorphose before my eyes into topazes, amethysts and rubies. One afternoon,

I am admiring a spectacular linden tree—the veins of its leaves expanding outward into delicate rococo designs, its flowers glistening like clouds heavy with snow—when I become aware of a noise behind me, shuffling and sly. My head swings toward it in one smooth movement; my body tenses, ready for confrontation. I take a few steps toward the shrub from which the noise originated, and two young boys emerge and sprint in the opposite direction, shouting as they run. I stand still as I watch them disappear, their muffled laughter echoing behind them.

Later that night, I turn out the lamps in the cabin and watch the darkness outside: waiting, ready. An hour passes, then another, but it makes no difference; I can wait all night if I have to. The crickets sing and I sit in the dark, seething and still.

As midnight approaches, I hear movement outside. Finally, those bushes are no longer an idle threat—for an instant, I feel vindicated. I position myself away from the windows, take a deep breath, and realize that I don't, after all, have a plan. I had vaguely imagined I might run out, make myself larger, frighten the intruders away. But I feel, all of a sudden, powerless; this is a moment I have been fearing for a long time. What is perhaps most surprising is that it took them so long.

The blows start to land, small at first, little rocks and stones. I hear them come closer, rummaging in the clearing, and I am incandescent with anger, both toward them and my own cowering helplessness. The rocks get heavier, the blows harder. A few hit the shutters and bounce off; they are chanting something, some kind of taunt. There are a few of them, all boys I think, older than the ones I saw earlier—on the cusp between childhood and adulthood, the most ruthless age. They move from the back of the cabin toward the front, and I hear them spurring each other on to greater acts of destruction; they laugh as they stamp on my flowers and rip up my plants.

The rocks resume, and after a few attempts one goes through a gap in the shutters—the glass disintegrates across the kitchen, covering the table and stove, shards all over the floor. They erupt into shrieks of glee, and I am ready to reach for my knife when another sound comes from outside: a clean howl. Then another, much closer. The boys go quiet; some of them attempt to make light of the situation but are shushed by the others. The clearing is still for a few moments—then, the sounds of fear, and the boys run away into the night.

Once several minutes have passed and my palpitations have subsided, I get up and unlock the door. In the moonlight the clearing is quiet, desolate. The chickens are nowhere to be seen. I kneel among the flower beds, the vegetable patch; in a few short minutes, the boys have devastated my garden, my riches— my companions. I stay hunched over the remains of the flowers, caressing the crushed fruits, the trampled vines, as though my touch alone could revive them. I look up at the sky, but the moon has vanished behind a cloud; I gaze out into the woods, but the wolf has disappeared.

For the first time in months, I do not sleep. As I lie in bed my fury intensifies until it is white-hot, blood burning through my veins. I wish I could—well, I am not sure what it is I wish for. It is more inchoate than that. Revenge and retribution whirl through my mind, but I know very well that there is no justice; a tragedy is not necessarily balanced out by something joyous. Beyond a certain point, when sympathy has fallen away, pain becomes distasteful to others, as if by venturing too close they might be caught in a vortex they will not be able to escape. It is catching, more deadly than any virus—it saps your humanity, little by little, until they no longer recognize you as one of their own. Day after day you become more transparent, until your materiality has trickled away and left behind a hazy and insubstantial outline, as though you were made of glass. But you do not stop feeling—that is the cruel trick—you are still there, as full of life and emotion as you ever were, waiting for them to see you.

I must show them I am not afraid. As much as I would like to live my life out here, it appears that I cannot completely sever my link to humanity—that time has not yet come. The village festival is a month or so away, and I shall attend with my head held high, be civil and charming. They will see that I harbor no malice, and will be thrilled by my anecdotes and quick wit. If you are there, in front of their eyes—fading, yes, but not invisible, not quite yet—it is more difficult for them to turn you into a monster with their words after you are gone.

4

In the morning, the clearing has begun to repair itself, but the pervasive damage is more evident than under the cover of darkness. I clear away the dead plants and do my best to revive the ones that have been trodden on; although I do not normally need to, I water everything with care. The kitchen is still covered in broken glass, so I bend down and painstakingly pick each fragment from the floor, shards piercing my skin. I try to go about my day as usual but my mood is foul; nothing seems to please me. I stalk about the cabin, then the woods, but everything appears flat today, the colors less vivid. I gaze at a tree and see nothing in it that enchants me.

Something is askew, the elements unsettled. I wander through the forest and sit on a log to gather my thoughts, absent-mindedly resting my eyes on a stone in front of me. But while my gaze is fixed on the rock, everything around it starts to move and mutate, objects unmoored from their solid state until it seems that they might rise up into the sky and drift away in odd directions. When I move my eyes from the stone everything jumps back into place, but I need only watch it for a few seconds more for the flowers and leaves to resume their uneasy dance. Perturbed, I look up at a nearby chestnut tree, hoping it will anchor me to my surroundings once again, but as I watch its strong and verdant boughs, its leaves appear to wither and die in front of my eyes, one by one, turning from green to orange to a dreary brown. Its branches become blanched and thin and crack away from the tree, which has turned skeletal and bare. I gasp and cover my eyes with my hands, curling up into a ball with my head between my knees, staying fixed in this position until the world has stopped spinning.

After several minutes like this, everything has gone quiet again, so I slowly unfurl and lift my head a little at a time. I open one eye and hazard a glance at the chestnut tree, which is upright and healthy once more, and I allow myself to breathe. Everything appears more stable, so I head back home before anything else goes awry.

In my absence, the crops' appearance has improved, but there is still a long way to go; it may take weeks for them to return to how they were before the attack. The chickens have returned and are pecking at the ground with a nervous energy. I give them a double helping of grain, to atone for last night's intrusion. I speak gently to the plants, assuring them, and myself, that all will be well. I water them again and go back indoors, locking the door behind me. I clean the kitchen to ensure no glass remains, tightly positioning a dictionary against the yawning crack in the window. I have a modest dinner before retiring for the night.

I can't sleep, still. The shadows across the ceiling shiver and shift; the wind has become louder, whistling through the branches. By now I should have become used to these eldritch scenes, but tonight my surroundings feel unfamiliar—as though my cabin were the same, yet subtly different. A thin draft wheezes through the gaps in the window, the glass rattling softly as it passes. I close my eyes and try to sleep, knowing that I will not. My body longs for relief but my mind refuses to let go, keeping the rest of me hostage with it. I toss from one side to the other but nothing feels comfortable; my eyes keep springing open. The room feels colder than usual.

Hours pass, and I am finally starting to drift into another realm when a creak wakes me. With an inhale of breath, I look toward the door—I locked it earlier, I made sure of that—but I stay very, very still. A fly buzzes near my head, a black dot hovering unpredictably in the air before settling on the fruit bowl in the middle of the table. Even though it is dark, I can see that the fruit in it has deteriorated rapidly since the afternoon, the banana stained by large, irregular spots, the fig blanketed in a layer of fuzzy mold.

And then, a step, in the corner of the room. I can barely breathe; my eyes are fixed on the fruit bowl in front of me. A shadow has appeared at the edge of my vision and is advancing slowly forward—a muffled step, then another one, closer. The stench fills my nostrils, a sweet, fetid smell of putrescent flesh, with a coppery undertone that turns my stomach.

By now, the figure is at the foot of my bed: standing, waiting. I can avoid it no longer. I let my eyes slowly rise up along its body—a man with a heavyset build, in a thick coat, a rifle slung over his shoulder. The left side of his body is covered in a dark, sticky substance. I close my eyes for a few seconds before directing them up toward his face. He has dark hair and an unkempt beard, dirt matted on his forehead, sagging skin shining as if with perspiration, one eye fixed on me, unblinking. The left half of his face is missing entirely: where the eye and nose should be is lacerated skin and exposed bone. Blood and pus drip from the wound onto his neck and coat and torso. Several more flies have appeared, one landing on his cheekbone, another disappearing into the grisly cavity.

I want to ask him why he has come home, why tonight. But I dare not move. So I lie there, motionless, returning his gaze. The night deepens, then begins to grow lighter. We watch each other until dawn, when my eyes flutter shut for a second and I drift into sleep. When I open them again, the room is empty.

*

The following morning is sunny, bright, as if nature itself is singing. But for hours I cannot stop shivering—something cold and insidious seems to have seeped into my bones. I think, just before vanishing, the figure said something to me—but I cannot for the life of me remember what, nor the sound of his voice. In the harsh light of day, I start to wonder whether it may all have been a nightmare—there is no trace of the intruder in the cabin, after all.

But there is one thing I cannot explain so easily. A clue *il mostro* left behind; evidence. I walk into the forest, a long way from the clearing, and when I find an isolated spot I begin to dig. Once the hole is large enough, I stand up and check that no one is around. Then I bury the decomposing fruits and the bowl that held them deep in the ground.

5

It has been weeks since the soldier stood at the foot of my bed, and no further visitors have come by. The plants and flowers in the clearing have grown almost completely back to how they were—some even more dazzling than before. My visions—or vision, I am not sure which is more accurate—but, this strange new layer that has become entangled with reality—all that has stabilized a little: a few gauzy swirls here and there, vibrant colors, the gentle pulsing of the earth. I did, at one point, think I saw a snow leopard peeking through the pines. But perhaps it was merely a lynx.

I can tell from the colors of the sky and the length of the shadows that the summer will soon come to a close: if I am not mistaken, the date for the festival is growing near. I inspect the calendar, attempting to guess which number on the page corresponds to the day outside my window. I do not wish to show my face in the village until the night in question, and so I begin today's walk by heading toward the most frequented path and wait for someone to come into view. I am just out of sight from the path—perfectly hidden—so that as soon as the occasion arises I shall stride out into the open, and it will appear as if I just so happened to pass there at that particular moment.

A few people walk past, but I do not like their faces. I am very sensitive, nowadays, to the demeanor of others—seeing as I so rarely meet with them, each encounter is laden with potential threats and pitfalls. Every exchange, no matter how cursory or insignificant, is sure to haunt my thoughts for days—weeks, if they are particularly unpleasant. And so it is vital that I choose the right person to ask. An elderly couple—no, too set in their ways, she seems diffident. A young family—the most easily panicked kind of all, they will not do. Three burly men—patently not right for the task at hand. And here he comes—a young man of unthreatening build, with a kind expression. The type who would jump at the chance to help an elderly lady carry her shopping—not that that is what I am, of course.

I slip out from behind the tree and amble—so casually—down the path toward him. My womanly wiles will help with this, I can tell.

"Good morning," I purr.

He starts, and stops. "Morning," he nods.

"You'll have to excuse me," I continue, putting on my most artless voice. "It's ever so distracted of me, but I seem to have forgotten which day of the week it is today." Men find it enchanting when women are in need of assistance, I have often found—especially when they do not know things.

He thinks for a second. "Wednesday? Wednesday, yes."

"Why, thank you," I flash him a captivating smile. Before he can move again, I add, "The eleventh, is it?"

He frowns, his stance stiffening. "No—uh—the twenty-fifth."

"Oh." I was a little off in my calculations, then. I inwardly reprimand myself—I had memorized the dates for the week, but the wrong week. "Well, that is very kind of you, young man." I curtsey—a nice touch, elegant—he is sure to be impressed. But when I look up he is hurrying up the path. I sigh: no manners. Or—maybe he was in a rush. Yes, let's say that.

I turn back on myself and return to the cabin, where the birds are glittering and the flowers dance as I approach.

"Hello, my darlings," I tell the peonies. "Good thing I checked the date with that kind gentleman—a few more days and I would have missed the festival."

"You're right," I say to the nasturtiums. "It would be a shame for them all not to see how much better I am."

"Why thank you, lilies of the valley. You do look rather radiant yourselves."

6

The next days pass in a whirl. I waltz around the woods and cabin, and tend to my crops with punctiliousness. I dig out my best dress—well, my second best—I cannot exactly attend the festival wearing the same outfit as last year—that would not do at all. I am known for my sophistication, you see, and we must all do our bit in the festivities. They shall be glad I have made an effort.

By mid-afternoon on Saturday, the soft hum of activity has started to swell, drifting up the mountain and into the clearing. I check the calendar again: today is the day. I practice my conversational opening gambits, the anecdotes I will tell—the forest has provided me with so many. I cannot wait to tell them all about my rhododendrons. Ladies like to talk about flowers, after all.

It has been a little while since I last washed my hair, but today is a special occasion. I might even put on a touch of makeup—not too much, though. I must think of my reputation. I dress and check my reflection, assuming first one expression, then another, as though I were conveying amusing gossip or engaging in serious discussion, perhaps throwing in a hint of coy flirtation, envisaging what the others will see. I appear rejuvenated in the mirror, perfected: my skin softly glowing, defined and graceful features, hair flowing behind me in handsome waves.

It is time: the sun is beginning to set, and people from all around are making their way into the center of the village. I say goodbye to the flowers and begin my descent, keeping my steps slow and regal, as though I were walking down the aisle.

Poise and comportment—that is essential. I stand tall, controlling each movement like a dancer whose body is her voice. The ground beneath my feet feels steady, strong; I feel its support as I emerge from the woods. I walk past the farm, the dog silent in its den, and then I am on the bridge.

When I am halfway across, I pause. I have not been here in months, and the noises coming from the streets in front of me are dizzying—loud and unruly and emanating from all sides. My old fears threaten to coalesce and overwhelm me, but I do not let them. I have changed, changed utterly. I advance and cross over.

At once, it is apparent that the general mood tonight is one of dissolution. The rich, sweet fragrance of smoke permeates the street, and singing is in the air; raucous, drunk already, overtly sexual in nature but with an undercurrent of aggression. Women make themselves available on street corners; rapacious men circle them like sharks, thinking they can mask their desire if only they move fast enough. Groups assemble, brandishing drinks that spill onto the pavement below, as though they could make the earth itself lose its shyness. Their laughter has a hard edge to it that gives away the true nature of their jokes.

I step past these boisterous groups, taking the long route. As I advance, I become aware of the usual stares from men—it is only natural—who turn and smirk at each other. I hear whispers, but do not listen to the words. I keep my steps steady as I walk, showing them I am not intimidated; if they wish to alarm me, they will have to do better than that. Streets and pavements are full, pullulating with life, but as I weave through the crowd I find that I do not need to elbow my way past; a pathway is opening for me as I go.

Passing through the narrow streets I stop for a few moments at the stalls on the way, to admire jewels and fabrics, toys and jars; I do not have any money, that is true, but it is polite to acknowledge the work people put into these things. I smile at the stall-holders, feeling magnanimous as I do so; having someone appreciate your work, really appreciate it, is surely as good as a sale—perhaps even more gratifying, to the true artisan. They smile at me, their gazes lingering as I leave.

As I go, I observe the faces of passers-by; if any meet my eye, I smile as if greeting a friend. Some groups go quiet as I approach—penitent about their past transgressions against me, no doubt; perhaps, there is also a little envy in their expressions. They are jealous of you, my parents would say when a schoolmate was unkind. And looking in the villagers' eyes tonight, I suspect they were right.

Closer to the center of the village, the signs of debauchery become rarer; here ages span from infant to crone, and a veil of dignity must be maintained. Family, they say, is the most important thing; in this part of the world, even the most committed libertine becomes cloyingly sentimental at that magic word. So they keep their sin at the gates, the sanctioned festivities suitable for those whose most iniquitous appetites have either abated or not yet developed.

It is here, outside the bakery, that I find a group I can attach myself to for a while. Enrico and Alberto see me first: the former stands back while Alberto comes up to me, tugging my sleeve. I bend down to stroke his hair, and he hesitates for a second before running to his mother. Well—he has always been shy.

"Signora Barbieri," I smile, extending a hand to her.

She nods, but does not take my hand—very impolite, I must say. I would have thought she had been better educated than that. But I will not let it show on my face.

"Signora Mantovani, what a pleasure." Her smile is tight-lipped—I would even go so far as to say it was strained. I had not thought we parted on such discourteous terms. Her husband is keeping his gaze on her, as if waiting for a cue as to how he ought to behave. The boys stand tentatively between them.

"And how are you enjoying the festivities, signor Barbieri?" I continue, addressing my question to him; if his wife is to be bad-mannered, it does not mean I shall descend to her level. I do not attempt a handshake this time.

"Very well, thank you," he says in a clipped voice. Not a conversationalist, this one. After a pause, he adds, "I hope you're keeping well?"

"Oh, splendid," I answer, although the answer should be self-evident. "I have my health. I walk in the mountains every day. What more could one want?" I laugh a peal of tinkling laughter.

I see now that his wife has her hands on each of the boys' shoulders, her fingers holding tight. She looks around her, as though she has forgotten my presence.

"Indeed—that is all anyone could need," he agrees; a wise man, and kind. "Well, have a lovely evening, signora Mantovani."

An abrupt ending, I must admit. I have not even told them about my rhododendrons. But so be it—I shall find better company.

"Wonderful to see you all." I bow toward them, a reminder of my refinement, and of whom they have just spurned.

I go onward into the night, admiring glances following me as I pass. I turn the corner and walk past the butcher's, reinvented as a bar for the night: a group is congregated around a small table, playing cards. People stand in doorways, smoking and embracing. After a few minutes I approach the entrance to the piazza, from the side nearest the church, and the wooden stage in front of the town hall comes into view. I stand for a minute and watch the disparate groups of people in front of me, wave upon wave coming from all directions, crashing against each other and dissolving, before forming new waves and dispersing again.

I had thought that the hordes of people tonight would have felt overwhelming after such a long absence from society, but as I watch the piazza I see with a curious clarity that perhaps I had been mistaken, that there is no division between town and forest, not really—I move with equal assuredness among both, for one thing. All I see appears as part of a greater whole, warmed by the same sun, refreshed by the same rainfall, supported by the same earth. As I look at the nonnas, the tearaway children, the stall-holders selling trinkets, I am suffused with an immense love for the people around me, with their habits and their foibles and their finely honed skills. This feeling, I am surprised to find, extends to everyone: Mrs Barbieri must have been expecting someone else—that is why she was distracted—yes, that must be right.

My face is now distended by a constant smile, as though I am blessing those around me, the young and old, weak and strong, peasant and landowner—all are beautiful to me. On the stage, a man and woman are singing; the sound reaches my ears haphazardly, lost in the whir of conversation and laughter all around. I wander through the crowd, taking in their faces and their spirit, and I am glad to finally feel at home—one of them.

I am engrossed in the sight of a mother and daughter playing together by the side of the fountain when the crowd begins to part, and I realize that the singing from the stage has ceased. Everything slows down, and when I look again at the crowd I notice that something has changed—something slight, almost imperceptible at first, but the more I look the stranger the sight appears. People are still staring, but their smiles are more crooked, less filled with kindness. The edges of their lips curl just so, wry amusement perhaps, with a shadow of cruelty; gazes appear more knowing. It is as though a dial has been turned too far, and too many things are happening at once.

The steps of the procession can be heard in the distance, the horns of the marching band, the rumbling percussion. But something is off—the sound is distorted, out of tune. Children scream all around, an insupportable cacophony of wails, indistinguishable from pain, that will seemingly never end. Instead of beautiful, the faces around me have become scornful: their features exaggerated, rough, each flaw accentuated. The laughter in the air brings with it no joy, but malice, a willingness to hurt. I feel dizzy—I need water. But the crowd is too tightly packed to move, and I do not wish to attract any more attention to myself.

That is when I notice an unusual phenomenon. It is not easy to tell when they are all moving around like this, but something is the matter with the way people look. Keeping my head still—perhaps if I do not move they will not notice me so much—I move my eyes from one face to another, trying to understand what is happening. As I watch a group in front of me, I notice a subtle flickering: people's faces, ever more grotesque now, seem to have developed an additional outline around them, a sinister halo threatening to take over from the faces they present to the world. Then one flickers—just for an instant—and the outline becomes real, more real than the face, before fading again into the shadows.

One flickers, then another, so that faces in the crowd become a scintillating mass, their corporeality quivering and fading in a flash before reappearing, an eerie light playing about people's heads. The flashes become longer, the apparitions more substantial—still too fast for me to make out what they are. The there and not-there seem to be clashing—I try to close my eyes, to make everything slow down. But I have not yet discovered how to control or curtail it—this thing that I am seeing. I have given it free rein for too long now. I cannot peel away the layers.

When I look again, the situation has worsened. The flickering is incessant, as though fireflies were dancing in front of my eyes; after a few moments they begin to blink in unison, then return to an aimless fluctuation. Some of the halos are starting to linger, and I frantically try to see what they are before they disappear again, my eyes darting from one face to the next. A man in front of me seems to be fading more and more into his shadow self, so I keep my eyes on him to wait for the next flicker. And there it is—a porcine snout emerging where his face should be, wide pink ears, tiny little eyes like dots—and it's gone, his face back, corpulent and drunk, lechery clouding his gaze. I continue watching him, and within seconds the monstrous hog has returned—bearing, I can see now, a distorted echo of the man's features.

One man standing opposite me, in policeman's garb, is replaced for a second by the form of a serpent, a bifurcated tongue flicking about his thin lips. A man with a jolly blond moustache, a teacher perhaps, appears faded, smudged—his lineaments morphing into those of a fearsome bull, waiting for the right opportunity to supplant them. A young woman behind him, modestly attired, flickers for the merest instant into a horned and bearded goat. I look around, and it is not just animals I see—there are demons, reptilian hybrids. One or two people, I think, turn for an instant into angels—but those flashes are too quick, too bright. For the most part, all I can see around me is malevolence and sin.

The procession is near now, the marching band's parping notes strident in my ears. I close my eyes again, minimizing the sensations entering my body; I take a few breaths, as slow and deep as I can. When I open my eyes the flickering has lessened, so I continue with my eyes closed for a while longer. The next time I open them, the flower girls have passed and soldiers are marching in precise formation, trampling the petals strewn on the floor. I watch their shining epaulets advance in unison, trying not to think about the ghostly figure at the foot of my bed.

It is the turn of the clergy, with their robes and their righteousness; above them, the statue of the Madonna and child, the gold canopy. I watch the Virgin Mary, baby Jesus, and turn my eyes to her other hand, the one holding the holy nail. I can see it much more clearly this time, now that I know what it is: long, almost as long as her forearm, surprisingly straight, sharp and covered in rust. I keep my eyes on it to avoid looking at the surrounding horde, and, as I watch the nail, everything around it begins to spin—as though the visible manifestations of things have become untethered from their true natures. They rise and dance in the air—then they begin to drift, outward, upward, spiraling out of control, and the only thing I can see is the nail as everything breaks down into molecules, drawing further and further away from each other, and nothing is between them except darkness and space and nothing, infinite nothingness, as though the universe itself were collapsing.

7

When I regain consciousness, it takes some time for shapes to come into focus. I close my eyes again, hoping I can make them all disappear, but the chatter swirls around me, louder and more insistent. I am on the ground, and someone is supporting my head and shoulders. I can hear footsteps, people calling for water. I know I must get up.

I open my eyes and see outlines assembled around me. The edges of my vision are still blurred, so I squint until I can make out faces and bodies and people again. They do not flicker this time, their features neither exalted nor grotesque; there is concern in their faces, and annoyance, and relief and amusement and boredom and after a second I realize that tears are streaming down my face. I have hurt my elbow in the fall; my head feels heavy. Someone passes me a glass of water, which I drink in small sips. Someone else is asking if I am all right.

I turn to see a man kneeling beside me, his hand on my forehead; he is asking questions, but I can barely take in what he is saying, much less formulate a response. An old woman in front of me is invoking a prayer to Santa Maria delle Grazie in a loud whisper, crossing herself as she speaks. I can feel the emotions of those around me more clearly now, a chorus of accusations— as though I had planned this, an undercurrent of fear; among them, there is curiosity, suspicion, awe, disgust. More whispers filter through to me: *santa*, *strega*, saint, witch. I wonder if the whispers are right, and if so which one.

I sit up higher, and things start to snap back into place. I assure the man next to me—the doctor, I can now see—that

I am well, and saying so makes me feel that it is true. He offers me his arm to help me stand, and I accept; when I am back to full height, I look around me at the people staring. But they are just people now. I feel drained of energy, like I could sleep for a week. I do not wish for a confrontation, so I extricate myself from the grip of the doctor and slip away into the crowd. As I hurry out of the piazza I see the apothecary watching me, his dark eyes serious and unblinking. I pass a large group, which moves to make way for me, and turn a corner into a side street.

People grow quiet as I approach. News of my collapse has traveled fast, with embellishments no doubt, the cause open to interpretation. I do not wish to hear their theories. I keep walking, looking at the ground as much as I can. I hear someone jeer something I wish I had not heard, see people whispering into each other's ears. And then I see him, in front of the butcher's, gazing on with the rest of the villagers. There is no warmth in his eyes, nor hatred, but a calm indifference, distancing himself from me once and for all; he has placed a protective arm around a young woman, soft blond hair framing her face.

My whole body feels heavy, as though my internal organs have been replaced with grains of sand; they appear to be trickling out of a hole in the bottom of my feet, so that soon there will be nothing left.

*

I sit on the bed, my back against the cool wall, and listen to the woods outside. Down in the village, the festivities have resumed, and the din of shouting and singing drifts through the air and into my clearing. The tropical flowers have gone, and the peacock; the few remaining vegetables and herbs have struggled in the heat. I have a little flour and oil left, and some water. I will need to chop more wood tomorrow.

As midnight draws near, I become aware of a splintering of the noise coming from below: a new, muted hum is spreading outward, into the woods. I step into the clearing and try to see what is happening, but the view in that direction is obscured behind the trees, so I lock my door and clamber up the mountain. Under the cover of the branches, the forest is quiet and still; out in the open, the moon is bright, suffusing everything with a soft, dim glow. I keep going until I reach an opening that overlooks the valley, where I see a hazy line of lights weaving through the forest. A candle-lit procession is ascending toward a tall group of pines.

A group, I can see now, is assembling under the trees. Lanterns have been placed in a circle around the surrounding clearing. The tallest tree—maybe not the tallest in the forest, but certainly the tallest within easy reach of the village—has been decorated with colorful paper streamers, red and yellow and gold. It is too far and too dark to make out individual faces; only vague movements are visible in the shadows. Gradually the group becomes larger, the chatter louder and more restless, heavy with anticipation as more people position themselves around the great trunk. I tighten my coat around me, shoulders shivering under the thin material.

Noises reach me in fragments: laughter, heated discussions, chants. Once everyone who needs to be there is present under the pines, the conversation fades away; a solitary male voice begins to speak, addressing the crowd in an authoritative tone. It is followed by a choir, somber and celestial, voices drifting airily up the mountain as though transported by a light wind. There is applause, another short speech; then a loud, sharp sound. After this the cheers begin, wild and unconstrained. The chosen tree in the middle of the clearing starts to rustle, its branches quivering against each other as its tip gently sways. For several minutes the cheers continue, rowdy and clamorous in the crisp night air.

A thud, and abruptly they cease. All is silent for a few terrible seconds. I strain to follow what is happening, but all I see are faint lights floating in the distance. A scream pierces the night, then another; candles and lanterns scramble toward the base of the trunk. There is shouting, raw and unpredictable. The pine tree has stopped rustling, standing preternaturally still amidst the turmoil.

I turn away and run back toward the cabin, my footsteps frantically crunching the ground. Behind me, the wails of women swell and surge until they fill the sky.

8

That night, I do not dream, but a sense of unrest greets me when I wake. I feel alert and vigilant, my ears pricked for the smallest sound, though I hear nothing out of the ordinary. Still, I am prepared: if they come, they will not find me waiting for them. But I hope it will not come to that.

I tidy the house from top to bottom, cleaning every surface and polishing each piece of furniture, dusting my books and folding my clothes. I find a flat, thin piece of wood and sand it down until it slots neatly over the window's broken glass. I go down to the well and fill several buckets over two trips, watering the crops to attempt to revive what is left. There are potatoes and runner beans, tomatoes and spinach; rosemary and sage grow wild. I forage berries and mushrooms from the woods. I slow down and savor each morsel, infused with the taste of the land. For a few weeks, at least, I shall have enough.

A day passes, then another, and I slowly adjust to my new, old surroundings. The sights of the forest fill me with neither ecstasy nor terror; I feel calm, resigned. I continue to walk, leaving as early as I can in the mornings and returning late at night. I climb to the summits and walk through the valleys; I meander through the woods, avoiding the paths. I keep an eye on the edges of things, to ensure they do not begin to waver, but everything stays in its place.

*

I am asleep one night when a thud stirs me from my slumber. My dreams seep through into my waking mind; I drowsily wonder whether it is Héloïse again, when I hear another noise, the muffled sound of men's voices.

I run to get my knife and crouch down next to the bed, under cover of the table. Outside, the moon is hidden behind thick clouds; the woods that surround the clearing are shrouded in darkness. I stay still, holding my breath, watching the windows, checking the shadows. All is silent; every crack and swish sounds like a death-knell. For a few minutes, nothing happens. I start to wonder whether I imagined the voices; my senses are not what they used to be. Then, a low figure passes in front of the window, stealthy as a snake. My heart is still for a second, then explodes in my chest. I grip my knife tighter, readying myself; my other hand holds the small glass bottle. Perhaps I am not ready, after all.

There is no singing this time, nor taunting; these are not adolescents. I watch every corner of the room, ears pricked for the slightest sound. After another minute, I hear a shout outside, a scuffle—growling. The tussle continues, more raised voices— there are at least three men. I stand up and run toward the front window, trying to stay out of the light.

The wolf has her jaws on one of the men's arms; he is screaming with pain, with rising panic. The others are shouting things at him, trying to hit the wolf with the butts of their rifles, but she holds on, until out of desperation one of them throws a knife at her. The wolf yelps and lets go, and as soon as the man has scrambled away one of the others has raised his rifle and—

The gunshot echoes through the clearing, so loud that for several seconds all I hear is ringing.

I cover my mouth with my hand, trying to stifle a yell. The men are laughing now, swearing, one bellowing in pain. "We need to go back," he is saying. "I'll bleed to death."

"All right, all right," says one of the others. "But we're taking this one with us."

Another gunshot; the yelps stop. Everything feels like it's spinning.

The man with the rifle kneels down and picks up the dead wolf, holding her over his shoulders. The other man helps the wounded one stand, and they head toward the woods.

After they have walked a few steps, the one carrying the wolf stops, then turns toward me.

"Hear that, *strega*? Next time we're coming for you."

9

I have read, somewhere, that a great deal of suffering might be spared if we were taught to expect nothing from the world in the first place. This had struck me as impossibly bleak at first, but the more I think of it, the wiser the proposition appears.

I am done, at last, looking outward for meaning, or knowledge, or acceptance. The more I look into the world, the more I realize I will not find these things there; it is through my own consciousness, flawed and deceitful though it is, that all is refracted. The sky, the clouds, the rivers are creations of my own mind, imperfect and biased approximations of their essential selves. It is my thoughts that give the outward world its qualities, its ability to hurt and delight—I would say in equal measure, but I am not so very sure. Like the spider, or the dreamer, I have weaved my life and now move in it.

Through desires, want is created; through need, lack. Little by little, I have turned down the noises roaring through my mind, slaked the thirst I had indulged for a variety of distractions. Everything feels quiet now, still. My thoughts no longer clamor for attention; I have no more desires, no more expectations, no physical craving, no emotional need. It is time for me to go home.

*

The next morning is bright and hard, the birds loud in the trees as if meeting again after a long separation. I go on my favorite walk, passing through the woods and the branches and up the steps until the paths widen out; the adrenaline is coursing through me as I reach the top of the pass. The air, the scents, the view come together as though part of a single organism, or rather revealing themselves as one. Everything is imbued with life and beauty, and I breathe it deep into my lungs.

In the afternoon I notice that my double vision has returned, a subtle extension of the real, the corners of things beginning again to multiply and expand in all directions, colors glimmering and full. I seem to be able to control it better now, dialing the intensity up and down, so that I am not overwhelmed. I feel connected to the forest like never before, as though I were part of the mountain, no more and no less than rock or tree or soil.

I go to the well, the bricks on its walls clear and pristine. I water the plants, then cook myself a flatbread with grilled vegetables. I watch the sun go down, turning the sky peach and lilac and pink before fading to a dark navy. I leave some food and water out for the birds.

Once the cicadas' shrill calls have grown quiet and the crickets have begun their nightly song, I know it is time to go. I take one last look around the cabin: everything is clean and tidy, my belongings in order. I pack a small bag with the things I will need, and leave my keys on the table before heading out into the night.

My boots crunch on the rocks as I ascend the mountain, the path familiar under my feet. The kerosene lamp lights a warm but unsteady glow around my immediate surroundings, but a gust of wind puts it out after a few minutes. I strike a match, then another, but they will not light; there is too much dampness in the air tonight. I discard the lamp and matches, and proceed upward.

Everything is blue and silver in the moonlight, small crystals on tree trunks and branches illuminating the way. The forest appears to part to allow me through; my muscles propel me instinctively along the path. A distant owl hoots from somewhere behind me, another responds up ahead. My eyes grow accustomed to the dim light; all is quiet except for the breeze and the rustling trees.

After another hour or so, I arrive at the pine tree at the top of the pass; the glade around it is calm. In the darkness, the tree's branches are black and strong, standing out darkly against its moonlit surroundings. I push my hand against the bark and breathe in the smell of the pine needles, which envelops me on all sides.

Out in the glade, a light wind has picked up; cool, but not bitter. I stand at the edge of the plateau and gaze at the valley below: from here I can see lakes, streams, villages, woodland, fields and pinnacles, some still covered in snow. The sky is black with night, the stars shimmer and glow in translucent formations, thousands of them, more dazzling than I have ever seen. I watch, and wait; I know something is coming, but I do not yet know what.

Minutes pass; the night deepens. Everything appears to be asleep. I do not move. And then, I see something in the distance: a haze is rising on the horizon, smoke perhaps, or mist. I hear a far-off rumble; the earth feels like it is moving. I close my eyes and take a deep breath. The air is thick, humid, as though it were about to rain; there is a tangy smell of iodine and salt. When I open my eyes, I start to see it.

It is coming in waves, over the mountains; small at first, rivulets of water dripping in through the cracks between the peaks, where the sky entwines with the land. It falls down the slopes and into the valley, where it swirls and spills against all it encounters. The waves get higher, stronger, sheets of water slide down toward the meadows and the lakes with a thunderous roar, engulfing everything below: the sea descends, ripping trees from their roots as it passes, ancient oaks and tender saplings, sweeping away rocks and shrubs as though they were dust, erasing rivers and streams into one mass of water. The basin expands outward, so that it forms a thin sheet of water all over the plain. Then the level starts to rise.

I call out, trying to warn those below, but the shout is lost in the night air; in any case, it is too late. The water is rising, wild and implacable, the waves crashing furiously over the side of the mountains like waterfalls, filling gorges and ravines. It is terrible and formidable. Greens and blues blend together, the sea of my childhood on one side, the Mediterranean on the other, then another, mightier, deeper, advances. The earth is grumbling beneath my feet, trees and branches thrash convulsively in the glade. The noise is almost deafening, booming like a foghorn through the still night air; up above, the sky is clear and unnervingly serene. The waves crest and swell and froth, white horses clashing violently before dissolving. By now the corrie is under water, whole towns have disappeared. I look down at the village and see it is about to be submerged in the raging tide.

Panic is rising in my throat; I shout as loud as I can. But I look again, and there it is, the there and the not-there, as though they were one. The village is inundated from all sides, from the lowest part of town, the piazza, the church, the café, powerful waves move toward the pharmacy, the outskirts, the bridge, the farm, my cabin. I see that beneath this veil the valley is in fact calm, the villagers asleep soundly in their beds. This is not reality, but it is no dream, either.

I am filled with a strange sense of elation as I watch the roiling sea below, flooding everything within sight. Beyond the mountains, I feel the billowing water rising and surging over all that is; I think of Héloïse and Antoine, Pierre and Marie, and realize that although we are apart we are united by something deeper than any of us understand, something still and golden and unchangeable at the core of everything that is. The waves are tossing and breaking against each other, forming small eddies; in the middle of the pool, the sea starts to bubble up, as if on fire, into the vortex of a shining whirlpool. The smell

©Alice Zoo

KATHRYN BROMWICH is a writer and commissioning editor on *The Observer* newspaper in London. She writes about all aspects of culture, including music, film, TV, books, art and more, and has contributed to publications including *Little White Lies*, *Dazed*, *Vice*, *Time Out* and *The Independent*. She has lived in Italy, Austria and the UK and is currently based in east London.

Acknowledgements

First of all I'd like to thank Eric Obenauf, Eliza Wood-Obenauf, Brett Gregory and the rest of the team at Two Dollar Radio for making this book possible. It's been a dream to work together and I'm so grateful for all your work and expertise. Thank you also to Tom Chivers and Roisin Dunnett at Penned in the Margins for taking a chance on this strange little novel in the first place. It's a shame things didn't go to plan, but without you the project would never have got off the ground.

Thank you to Matt Turner for championing the novel from the start, and for your sharp, thorough and insightful edits, which teased out hidden aspects of the story I hadn't even noticed were there.

Thank you to Jane Ferguson and the *Observer New Review* team for being so consistently brilliant, and for your continued patience and support during my convalescence from long Covid.

Thank you to Tina, Vicki and Martine for reading a draft of my terrible speculative fiction novel and for your helpful feedback, which was instrumental in coming up with a better idea. Thank you to Hannah for reading an early draft of this and providing some encouragement at a time when I needed it. Thank you to my friends for being generally excellent and keeping me sane.

Thank you to my parents, William and Franca, for your steadfast love and support over the years. It means everything to me.

And finally thank you to Adam, for being nothing like the husband in the story. I couldn't have written the book without you (and the cats).

of the sea is in my nostrils and the wind is in my hair, and I feel terror and peace, awe and consternation, and all the feelings I have ever felt pass through me as though for the first time, the pain and the joy, all the faces I have ever seen; past, present and future are happening, all at once, when the world was water, and will be again; my sense of self falls away and I am aware of something vast inside me, and outside, and all of a sudden I know things, things that cannot be put into words—I see all, and I feel all, the streets are rivers, waves crashing on the panes, water is everywhere, burning green and blue and white, on the clod of clay and the pebble of the brook, we are one, all is one, the mountain and the sky and all that surrounds us, trembling and wild.

I look out at the view, and I feel everything.